LAW
IN
FLAMES

LEE DION

PAGE PUBLISHING, INC.
Conneaut Lake, PA

First originally published by Page Publishing 2021

ISBN 978-1-6624-4331-2 (pbk)
ISBN 978-1-6624-4333-6 (hc)
ISBN 978-1-6624-4332-9 (digital)

Printed in the United States of America

WHILE THIS NOVEL is a work of fiction, it is based almost entirely on real events which took place over the long career of one amazing and remarkable man—James Fetterly. This is, in essence, his story, and the book is dedicated to the memory of his incredible accomplishments.

Jim was a leading expert attorney in the field of fire litigation. His entire life and legal practice were dedicated to bringing justice and equity to the parties who suffered catastrophic loss resulting from disastrous fires. His work stands alone, pioneering in the presentation of scientific and forensic evidence. Jim's ability to bring clarity and humanity to the courtrooms, juries, and legal proceedings is unprecedented.

Much of his success can be attributed to major factors—scientific rigor and a masterful ability to communicate. Those factors created such a demand he was often called upon to give seminars, teach, and mentor.

Jim was a deeply committed man, reverent, family-oriented, gracious, and caring.

It is out of respect for these qualities and not just his career accomplishments that we remember James Fetterly. It is my hope this novel will give the reader a feeling for his remarkable life; for it is the man who inspired this book and not just his amazing story.

Acknowledgments

I AM INDEBTED to my wife, Micki, for her encouragement and her excellent editorial skills. I am grateful to Judy Fetterly, Skip Patterson, and Rick Natkin for their aid in character development and narration.

PART ONE

HAPPY NEW YEAR

1

December 31, 1986
San Juan, Puerto Rico

WAVES GENTLY WASH over the sands of an idyllic tropical beach. Playa San Juan Hotel brochures boast their luxurious resort hotel is one of the premier hotels in the entire world, and they are correct. Ask any of the contented guests lolling around on the strand. The Playa San Juan is a favorite escape from the cold winters of Canada, the US mainland, and even Europe. And for New Year's Eve, the Playa San Juan is booked solid.

It is around eleven a.m. right now, and most of the folks enjoying the beach at this hour are families with children. Pasty white adults holler at their rowdy kids, already crimson with blooming sunburns as they dig sandcastles, splash in the gentle waves, and run hog wild. That's okay. Parents like Ed and Angie Samuelson of Kalamazoo, Michigan, are more than happy to let their kids, Mikey and Maggie, ages five and three, wear themselves ragged. In fact, Ed and Angie are counting on their children to conk out exhausted by midafternoon. The kids already love Idalia Romero, the babysitter they hired through the hotel, like a grandmother. She's a big-hearted, energetic woman, full of love, with a twinkle in her eye. They trust her to watch over the kids, who will drop off into naps soon after they return to the room in midafternoon. Then Ed and Angie will be free to enjoy each other and celebrate the hotel's New Year's Eve bash, free of worry. Just the two of them, for once. They chose the Playa

San Juan for this vacation partly because it is practically notorious for unbridled intensity when it comes to auld lang syne. This place is getting ready to party down, big time, and so are they.

If you look back from the beach at the Playa San Juan, the high-rise hotel soars twenty stories above one of the nicest stretches of prime beachfront real estate in San Juan. On the right, the hotel's luxurious casino has a clear view of the sea, thanks to the largely glass walls on three sides. Not that anyone goes in there to gaze at the beach. The casino boasts a variety of gaming options to rival anything in Las Vegas: poker, blackjack, roulette, baccarat, etc. If you like to bet the farm on the turn of a card, this could be your chance.

Prefer roulette? The wheel never stops spinning, day or night. Or if your thing is dice, you can roll the bones at one of the craps tables. Even the nickel slot junkies have plenty of one arm bandits to keep them busy. Or if you're a bigger player, there are machines for dimes, quarters, dollars… Up to you to decide how much and how fast you want to blow through your nest egg. The action is constant, the floors and ashtrays always being cleaned, and the beautiful young women passing out free drinks are in continuous circulation.

Now, back to our vantage on the beach. Take a look over to the left, at the attractive modern structure next to the casino, separated by an open atrium. This is the ballroom complex, two stories of expansive floor space, also featuring walls with lots and lots of glass to enjoy the magnificent view of the beach and the sparkling ocean beyond, at least when the curtains are open. Although they are often closed, especially when the daytime sun threatens to turn them into saunas the size of airplane hangars.

Not to worry. Plenty of air-conditioning for both the casino and these expansive ballrooms. Most of the year these facilities are in full swing, hosting business meetings, medical conferences, and conventions of every stripe. And why not? Who wouldn't want to attend a convention (or a wedding, for that matter) inside the Playa San Juan's well-appointed ballroom facilities while staying at this posh resort and casino at the edge of the sea? Sure beats Cleveland. The ballrooms can be subdivided to suit the size your group needs and catered by a world-class cuisine from the resort's kitchen. It's no surprise ballroom venues are booked solid most of the year.

But not now. Not in December. Not at the peak of the resort's high season, when all the guest rooms are booked at rack rate (and not the reduced charges a convention can negotiate). No, during the Christmas season, the ballrooms generally stand empty and unused while the rest of the hotel is virtually teeming with activity, filled with snowbirds, catching their dose of tropical paradise instead of shoveling their driveways.

Shoveling the driveway is one thing Jim Feller could do without. But that's December for you here in Oakmont, Wisconsin. Jim is just glad to be home again after a grueling (and successful) six-month litigation. The case kept him busy 24-7 in San Francisco and away from home the whole time. Jim's the best in the business when it comes to the huge complexities and massive dollar damages that are at risk in major fire claims. It's a very discreet and high-dollar niche in the field of corporate liability law, and Roberts, Davies, and Feller is the premier firm in the field for one reason: over the last two decades, Jim Feller has built a reputation as *the* man to handle your fire-loss case—whether you are the defendant seeking to limit your liability for the staggering losses of a major commercial fire or the plaintiff seeking recovery after catastrophic, often existential, damage to your business.

What makes Jim uniquely endowed to dominate his specialized area of practice? Yes, he's a charismatic, charming advocate in the courtroom. He is ruggedly handsome and impeccably dressed, but in a way that is so understated even a blue-collar juror will be comfortable with him. He projects tremendous intelligence, yet he manages to come off as compassionate and plainspoken, even amiable. No matter how complicated the evidence, and regardless of how technical the expert testimony becomes, Jim has a way of leading a jury though the wilderness. He never makes the them feel that he is talking down to them or trying to be too clever by half. He never appears manipulative or condescending, as so many attorneys can't help doing. There are a thousand reasons for this: an incredible amalgam of skills, knowledge, humanity, thoroughness, and credible believability. He always gives the impression he's the smartest guy in the room yet somehow manages to make you believe he doesn't even know it, let alone push it in your face. Juries naturally find him trustworthy, and for a good reason. He is trustworthy.

But all these things are not what puts Jim at the top of this game.

No, Jim's most valuable quality in the courtroom is that he is a master storyteller. He can lead a jury from beginning to end, setting up even the most complex arguments in a way that makes it all feel simple. He can paint a picture the jury can actually see. He sets up a simple, logical framework to support his overwhelming mountain of detailed evidence. He enables a juror to follow every tiny detail of a baffling jigsaw puzzle he fits together, piece by piece. He makes a jury feel like they are watching Jim start with a beautiful, bare Christmas tree and then shows them where to hang every ornament, every twinkling light, every precious decoration made by children now grown. He makes it all fit. And by the end, the entire and unitary whole appears as a logical product of the details in evidence. Jim can not only lead a horse to water, he can make the horse understand the cure for thirst. The rest just falls into place.

Over the years, Jim has built a reliable team of scientific and forensic experts and helped devise experiments that prove not just how a fire starts but how it kills. His landmark demonstrations have led to more than just courtroom victories. His compelling narratives have extended industry and government understanding about the dangers posed by toxic materials when they catch fire. His work has established fact patterns that form the basis for regulations which have saved countless lives.

This kind of success comes with costs. The dedication to put in countless hours, often in far-off cities, for extended absences can send quality family time up in smoke, as it were. Julie met Jim in college and married him while he attended law school. She knew right from the start how much time his voracious study habits could consume. She understood the brutal hours required of a junior associate who wanted to make partner. Yet Julie has never had a doubt about Jim's devotion to her or their children, Ellen and Sarah. Often he was trapped on an extended trial out of town. Yet he spent hours on the phone with Julie and the girls. He took red-eye flights home for so many weekends. Anytime the girls were on a school break, Jim would rent a fabulous house or condo and then fly the family out for a vacation to spend time with him.

But there were so many things missed, times that can never be replaced: missed birthdays, missed school plays, missed soccer games and tennis matches and swim meets, holidays, anniversaries.

This year Jim hoped his case in the Bay Area would be all wrapped up by Thanksgiving. But as settlement issues dragged on, he wasn't home to carve the turkey. He did manage a break for Christmas, flying home to Wisconsin December 21, in time to greet the girls when they got back from college (Oberlin for Ellie and Sarah flying up from Tulane). Jim spent every possible moment with Julie and his "college girls." But on Boxing Day (Julie, a lifelong Anglophile, loves calling December 26 Boxing Day), he has to fly back to San Francisco. The final settlement is signed off on the twenty-eighth. Jim's set to fly home on the twenty-ninth, but a blizzard shuts down every airport from Des Moines to Sandusky, paralyzing the whole Midwest, including Wisconsin.

So it isn't until December 30, 1986, that Jim finally makes it back to home his sweet home in Oakmont, the suburban gem of Milwaukee, just in time to get up on the frigid morning of New Year's Eve to shovel the damn driveway. But it's worth it because Ellie and Sarah pitch in as Julie keeps up a steady flow of hot cocoa. What matters is, they are all together.

Jim is glad for the help. The sooner they finish, the sooner they can start getting ready for the New Year's Eve festivities they have planned for tonight.

2

December 31, 1986
San Juan, Puerto Rico

"Yo, Luis? Going to the meeting, bro?"

"For what?" Luis Ortiz doesn't look up from the oysters he is shucking. That's a good way to lose a finger.

"The vote, man. On the new contract?" Manny has to yell over the noise of the power spray nozzle in the big steel sink where he is washing dishes. He's a skinny, talkative kid, three months on the job in the hotel kitchen and starting at the bottom.

"So?" Luis says.

"What you mean, 'so'? This our new contract, man."

"Es mierda." Luis shakes his head in wonder.

Was he ever that dumb? Maybe twenty years ago, when he was washing dishes himself, like Manny Huerta is now. Luis is forty-four, spent half his childhood living in Miami, even has two years in a Florida junior college. But at twenty-one, he was home to visit his auntie and uncle. And he met Effie, a shy country girl so beautiful she made Luis ache for her so much he moved back to Puerto Rico to marry her. Twenty-three years, four kids, and forty-five pounds later, Effie is still a shy, religious, conservative woman, even more pious than ever, if that's even possible. He still loves her, Luis would say. But put a couple drinks in him, and Luis might admit that Effie is not the girl he left Miami for, not anymore. But Luis works hard for his family, always has. A steady, decent job in the resort kitchen at the Playa San Juan, where he has slowly worked his way up. He's the head Sous Chef now. *Five years, or maybe only four, when old Hector retires, this is going to be my kitchen,* he thinks.

He is careful to keep his eyes focused on his work with the oyster knife as he answers the kid over his shoulder, "I got a lot to do, junior. So do you."

"I'm good, bro. I got it under control." Luis knows Manny is attacking the endless piles of dishes and staying ahead of the buildup. For now.

"This is your first New Year's Eve, right, Manny?"

"Yeah, and I got a hot mama all lined up tonight. Can't wait to get my ass outta this kitchen."

"When's your shift up? Six?"

"'S'right, brother. And I'm gonna party big time tonight." Manny does a little cha-cha move, grasping his package and thrusting his hips.

Luis shakes his head. "You wanna see any pussy tonight, you better have every fucking dish in this place cleaned, dried, and stacked."

"I'm all over it, Cheffe."

"Who's your relief?"

"Ordonez? I think so anyway."

Luis groans. Ordonez is okay, when he's sober. But what are the chances of that on New Year's Eve?

"Ay, that *hijo de perra*? Busiest night of the year, and I get that *boracho* to worry about."

"Won't be your worry. Ain't you off at six too?"

Luis snorts. "Off duty, yeah. But I can't leave. Not on New Year's."

"Why not?"

"Gonna be a zoo tonight, I told ya. Somebody's gotta keep this shit show on the tracks."

"Aah… You just like bitching. I know you're going for the holiday overtime."

"*Que te den.* You'll see. One day you'll have a family."

"When I do, I ain't planning to leave my wife alone on New Year's Eve."

Luis ignores this. He's got plans for New Year's Eve too. Only they don't include his wife, Effie.

"Just make sure you don't leave nothing extra for Ordonez."

"Don't sweat it. When I get back from the meeting, I will go into overdrive."

"*Carajo*. No, skip that *mierda* meeting. You got too much work to do."

"Yeah, but Rosa told me we get an hour off to go vote. Paid time too, he says. No clock out."

"Ah, Rosa. That full-of-shit *hijo de puta?*" Luis grits his teeth. If he gets the kid in hot water with Rosa, the union will start to fuck with him, or this whole kitchen staff more likely. "*Mierda*. If you ain't done at six? Your ass is staying until I say."

"Bro, bro. Do I ever let you down?"

Luis smiles. Not a bad kid, Manny. Not a fuckoff, anyway. Shows up. Does his job.

"Tell you what, kid," Luis says to him. "Take your paid hour off. Go grab yourself a beer, have a smoke. Enjoy life. But don't waste your time at no union meeting."

"Yeah, well… I told Rosa I'd go. He's counting on me, he says."

Efrain Rosa, Luis thinks. Lazy Union jerkoff. He's a skilled butcher and a very handy fellow with a knife. *But* he's never *around* when the kitchen's busy. Still, there's no getting rid of the asshole. A real *lame botas*, he's all juiced in with Beltran and the other Union bosses. They're even gonna make Rosa a shop steward, word is. Fucking Teamsters. Bunch of crooks.

"Fine. You wanna waste your time listening to those guys jack everybody off? Do it. Be my guest. But don't count on any contract. Not yet."

"That's why we're having the meeting. Rosa say they're really close."

Luis can't hold back a scoffing laugh.

"What? You think I'm funny?" Manny asks, defensive, a little hurt even.

Luis is sorry. Kid's just naïve. He'll learn. He softens his tone.

"I don't mean nothing personal, son. I'm just letting you know how things shake down around here, that's all. Go to the meeting or don't. I'm just saying, we're going on strike either way. Count on it."

"Rosa told me the hotel is ready to make a deal."

"I'm sure they are, kid. They sure as hell don't want any walk-out, 'specially in high season."

"So then…" Manny shuts off the spray. "You ain't making any sense. If the hotel wants to settle, why would we strike?"

"Because this year it's our turn. It was Hilton last year. Two years ago, it was…Sheraton, I think. This is just the way it works."

"Yeah, but…what do you mean, it's our turn? I mean, we're all Teamsters, right? All the hotel workers. Why us?"

"It's the way Teamsters work it. They got all the hotel workers organized. All of us paying our Union dues every paycheck, right?"

"No shit. Big-time bite they take, bro."

"Yeah. So like at the end of the year? All the hotel contracts end at midnight. Every year, just like tonight. No new contract? All the hotel workers walk off the job. Happy New Year, right?"

"Yeah, but we got to vote first. If we pass the new contract—"

"Ain't gonna happen." Luis chuckles. "That's why this vote, this whole damn meeting? Just bullshit as usual. I'm telling you, come midnight? We're going out on strike."

"But…why?"

"It's our turn this year, that all."

"That don't make any sense."

"Wrong, junior. Think it through." But the puzzled look on Manny's face tells Luis he has to spell it out for the kid. "Works the same way every year. Listen, Roberto Beltran? You know who that is?"

"No…"

"He's our president. Teamster Local 901. That's us, all of us, the hotel staffs at every major hotel in Puerto Rico."

"Yeah, I know. We're all Teamsters."

"And every December our contract runs out at the end of the year. So Beltran and his crew, they sit down to work out a new deal with the hotels. Nobody wants all the hotels closed down."

"Right. 'Course not. That's why we need to vote—"

"Sure, sure. Nobody wants a strike. Bad for the hotels. Bad for the Teamsters Union too. Nobody's paying dues if they're all out on strike, right?"

"Well, yeah… And we don't get paid nothing either."

"Sucks all around, right? So here's the deal. Instead of sending out everybody all at once, Beltran picks one hotel. Different one each year. It's us this year, but everybody gets a turn. So next? Beltran sits down to hack out a deal with the Playa San Juan. We're the one on the chopping block this time around. If Beltran don't get a deal he likes from Playa San Juan, he takes us out on strike."

"Just us? What about—"

"The other hotels? That's the beauty, kid. All the rest, they keep working. Temporarily, under the old terms, until a new contract gets settled."

"Except us? But we're getting screwed!"

"Ain't about us. It's Playa San Juan gets the real fucking over. They're shut down. Beltran still has most of the Teamsters working. Dues coming in and all that, right? He's fine with that."

"Why does that make sense?"

"Because there's still fifteen, twenty other hotels all doing business as usual. They're making money. Their people are getting paid."

"And we just get kicked in the *cajones*?"

"We get a little something. Strike benefits, if it keeps going. But it won't."

"How do you know? We could be out for months."

"Can't happen. See, if it's just Playa San Juan getting screwed? They're gonna fold. What choice do they got? With all the other hotels still open? Taking in all the tourist business, high season, making coin while Playa San Juan sits empty? Nah, they gotta cave in, or they go broke. And once Beltran gets what he wants from Playa San Juan, that's the new standard. The rest of them fall in line. They all sign the same deal, and life goes on."

"Yeah, but…"

"It's leverage, son. That simple. And this year, Playa San Juan is the sorry-ass goat that gets slaughtered. Our turn. That's the program, kid."

"Yeah, but…" Manny frowns with concentration. "Suppose Playa San Juan's offer is good enough. I mean, what if we say yes?"

"Can't happen. Don't matter what Playa San Juan offers. Beltran will tell you guys it's no good, and you saps will all vote to strike. Then come the end of next week, Playa San Juan folds, they sign off, and all the other hotels are stuck with it."

Manny thinks on that, then he smiles. "That's pretty smart, ain't it?"

"For Beltran? Yeah. Him and the Teamster bosses make out great. Same as every year."

"Yeah. And so do we. Right?"

"We end up with a little pay bump. Maybe. But mostly the hotels end up paying more dough into the Teamsters pension fund. Or maybe the *Beltran-wants-a-new-house-with-a-bigger-fucking-swimming-pool fund*. Point is, money changes hands, all right. But not much of it trickles down to our hand, kid. It goes into the Local, and the Local kicks up to the International Brotherhood of Teamsters. And that's that."

"Well, but…like the Pension Fund? I mean, we get that eventually, don't we? Like retirement benefits and shit?"

Luis laughs so hard he has to stop opening oysters or he'll lose a thumb.

"Kid, once that money goes into the Teamster pension fund, nobody ain't gonna see it again. It's long gone, just like Jimmy Hoffa."

"Who's he?"

Luis hears somebody coming in through the kitchen's back door.

"Hey, you fellas?" Luis doesn't stop cutting open oysters or look up. He already knows who's talking. "Meeting is on for three this afternoon. In the lower ballroom. Be there," so says Efrain Rosa, teamster stooge; but with an oyster knife in his hand, Luis isn't dumb enough to say that out loud.

3

December 31, 1986
Oakmont, Wisconsin

As Jim FINISHES knotting his tie, he notices his wife, Julie, crossing the room behind him in the mirror. And for a second, he is stunned just by the sight of her. Twenty-two years married, and he can't see much difference from the athletic, shapely, and vigorous girl he fell hard for. Long legs, tumble of ash-blond hair (well, the odd gray, who's he to talk?), same willowy build she was blessed with before the two girls. Partly the tennis, he figures. She's nuts for it, plays indoors all winter. But sometimes it still amazes him how she can just take his breath away. Smart as a whip too and teaches English at the local high school.

"Julie?"

"Not now, Jim. I can't find that pin you gave me from last Christmas."

But he can't help staring at her.

"You are…such a knockout."

Julie looks up from the drawer she's rifling. "Sorry? What?"

"You heard me." He crosses the room and wraps his arms around her. "Sometimes I just… I don't believe I'm so lucky, that's all."

"Aww." She blushes then gives him a short kiss on the cheek. "You're sweet. Now turn me loose so you can take me to the party and show off your prize."

Jim holds her a little tighter. "Maybe I just want you all to myself tonight."

"Well…" she says, a coy tone creeping into her voice, "nothing says we can't leave the club early." Now she returns a real kiss. Then she adds, "The girls both have dates too. They'll be out until all hour—"

"Mom, I found it—" Oops. Sarah bounds in, the lost pin in her hand. Hard to say who is more embarrassed, Sarah or her parents. The instant she comes in, they are moving apart with matching expressions that scream, *Clinch? What clinch?*

Julie turns her attention to her daughter and the pin like it is the greatest treasure on earth, and her life is saved.

"Oh, darling. Thank you so much."

"Uh…sure." She starts backing out. "And, uh, you look great, Mom."

"Thanks, sweetie."

"Have fun, you guys," she tosses in, making a break for the door before her burning cheeks catch fire.

But before her escape is complete, Julie clears her throat and says "Sorry, I missed that. Did you say, *'You too, Dad'?*"

Sarah glances back at Jim. "You look…uh…perfect, Dad. As usual."

"Thank you," Jim says, brushing at his lapels.

"If you're on your way to argue at the supreme court."

Jim glances back at his image in the mirror. Bespoke three-piece suit, a nearly black shade of dark-gray, bright-white tailor-made shirt with catchy onyx-and-silver cuff links, Ferragamo shoes buffed to a blinding shine, and a silk tie that costs more than your average set of white wall radials. *Yeah,* he realizes. *Maybe just a tad overdressed for a New Year's bash.*

"Think the tie is a little…gaudy?"

"Gaudy?" Julie laughs. "Sweetie, you are so not gaudy. You make Johnny Cash look colorful."

"I could pull out that Hawaiian shirt from Maui."

Julie steps back and looks at her man, shakes her head. "Just leave the vest and put on some comfortable dancing shoes."

"Yes, Teacher."

4

Playa San Juan
December 31, 1986

IT'S ONLY ABOUT half past two, and already the hotel casino is churning like a zoo. Sofia Ocasio regrets wearing the spiked heels, even though she always makes a lot more in tips when she does. And the heels sure seem to be working today. She hasn't once made it all the way from the service bar to the far side of the slot machines before she is so swamped with cocktail orders she has to turn back. Jose Nuñez is jumping all over it at the service bar, can't keep up, but he's doing his best. Sofia, for that matter, can barely keep count of the tip money she keeps sweeping up. So much money it excites her.

And that excitement starts to kindle a different heat inside her, one unrelated to her hectic travels back and forth on the crowded casino floor. She is already aroused by a sensuous dreaminess, anticipation over her plans to hook up with her secret lover after her shift ends at eight this evening. But the way her motor is running already, she doesn't think she can wait that long. Maybe it's the sense of wanton hedonism permeating the atmosphere of the whole casino. The sprawling room rocks with overstimulated customers, already in full party mode and on the verge of cutting loose in unbridled enthusiasm. Maybe it's the spell of New Year's Eve. *Or*, she thinks, *maybe I'm just horny.*

She drops her tray off at the bar, along with a slip of drink orders people have pressed on her. But Sofia tells Jose not to fill her order yet. She's going to take a short break.

"No problem, chica," he tells her. "Take your time. My arms are falling off anyway."

On her way toward the kitchen, Sofia ducks into the ladies' room and touches up her lipstick. It's a little joke between them. He always tells her to be careful; he doesn't dare get any lipstick on his kitchen whites. And Sofia loves to tease him about it. But in the back of her mind, there's a little part of her that wouldn't be too sorry if his wife did catch him. Maybe then he would leave that fat, old bag like he keeps saying he wants to.

Sofia has to walk carefully when she goes into the huge kitchen. Last week she got one of her sharp heels caught in one of the little holes in the rubber safety mat. She turned her ankle, which was all the more infuriating because the whole point of the goddamn mats was to keep people from slipping on wet floors. Anyway, she steps more carefully now, moving through the relatively calm kitchen. Although there are always a couple of the hotel restaurants open at any hour, it's well past lunchtime, and nobody is going to be looking to eat dinner for a few hours at least.

As she passes her man, deliberately ignoring him in case anyone notices, Sofia lets a wicked smile play across her freshly done, shiny red lips. She sees him glance up at her, knows he is following her with his eyes, watching her as she makes her journey all the way to the supply room at the far end of the kitchen, way in the back. She opens the door and disappears into the enormous storage pantry filled with aisle after aisle of nonperishable supplies, everything from silverware to canned goods, concentrated soup stocks, a wide variety of spices, condiments, glassware, teabags, sugar and salt and pepper, and spices of every kind. She stops when she gets as far as she can from the entry door and listens.

It's less than a minute until she hears the door open and then the sound of his voice. It is always deep and rich. That was the first thing she noticed about him, that sensual sound that made her feel weak with need, without even caring what words he was saying.

"I sure hope you aren't here to tell me our date is cancelled."

"No… I came to say… I don't think I want to wait that long. If you can take a little time now, that is." As he comes around the edge of the aisle, she can see that Luis is already taking off his apron and pulling at his shirt. She has already stepped out of the short, tight skirt that inspires so many tips while she peddles cocktails. Just before his hands find her, he warns, "Just try not to get that fucking lipstick all over me this time, Sofie."

Luis hates the term "quickie." Nothing about making love to Sofia should be quick, he thinks. Which is why he is still looking forward to their date tonight. He told Effie, his plump and uninterested wife, that he would be doing a double shift for New Year's Eve, won't be home until past midnight. By that time, he expects Effie will have been snoring for hours. In fact, Luis plans to work past his shift's end at six tonight. Then he will hang around the casino until Sofia gets off work at eight, enjoying the free drinks she brings him. Once she's off, they will have several hours together at her apartment, which is only a five-minute walk from the Playa San Juan.

But this little afternoon delight doesn't dampen his pleasant anticipation for the evening. If anything, watching her step back into her thong, it seems to be the perfect appetizer. Now he looks forward to a long, lazy meal tonight. Before she can wriggle back into her tight skirt, he puts his hands on her fine, round buttocks and pulls her against him. He puts as much bass into his voice as he can manage because he knows how it turns her on.

"I can't get enough of you. You know that, don't you?"

"You'll get all you can handle tonight, I promise. But I better get back to the casino before too many Yankees die of thirst."

"That's okay. I have another ten dozen oysters to open for tonight."

"Make it eleven, and eat a dozen for yourself," she teases.

"For you, I won't need them," he rumbles, and then he is pressing his mouth against her lips, knowing he will have to do another cleaning job with another fresh napkin.

Thank God for the linen supplies.

Just as their mouths part, they both freeze at the sound of the supply room door opening again. *Shit,* he thinks. *The last thing I need is to be caught in here boinking a cocktail waitress. Especially after that problem two years ago with the coffee-shop cashier. Sofia doesn't even know about that one. It was before she came to work at the Playa San Juan.*

He puts his fingers to his lips, warning her to silence, although he knows he doesn't really have to. She doesn't want to get caught either; she isn't even on an official break. And she loves the fat tourist tips she is making here.

They both crouch down low, and Luis hears the squeak of a rolling cart. Whoever is coming in here, they must be planning to load up quite a lot of something. *It better not be something back here,* he thinks.

It's not. The cart squeaks its way to only the second row and stops. Now he can hear whoever it is heaping a whole lot of small items onto the cart. It sounds like they are all of the same size, and not very big, judging by the small clicks as he stacks them. Cans, they must be. Some kind of small cans. He tries to think of what kind of small cans this guy would be packing onto his cart. When he thinks about it, most of the canned items in this supply room are huge, like five or ten-pound cans of tomatoes, or beans? It also occurs to Luis that this person didn't seem to look around much, didn't have to hunt to find what he came in here for. So it must be someone who knows their way around this kitchen and the supply room.

He chews on that for a moment. True, he doesn't want to be caught *in flagrante dilecto* with Sofia, boinking in the back room. On the other hand, he holds a position of responsibility in his kitchen, a position he has worked for many years to achieve. Maybe there's a perfectly good reason that someone is here piling up little cans of…whatever. But a month doesn't go by where Luis doesn't discover some kind of pilferage and have to fire another thief.

Motioning for Sofia to stay down and keep out of sight, he edges closer, putting himself in a position to at least get a glimpse at whoever is raiding the pantry when they finally finish loading up and head for the door. Depending on how things work out at that point, he will either see an innocent reason for some employee to be stocking up on something for a legitimate reason or he will catch a thief red-handed.

It is only a few more moments before that squeaking wheel tells Luis the cart is moving again, heading for the door. The cart comes into view. And then he sees who is pushing it, although they are in profile, and then quickly passes, so he only sees the back of their head. But clearly this person doesn't see Luis at all, doesn't know he's been observed.

Luis feels a painful, hot burst of acid flood his stomach. He doesn't know why fucking Efrain Rosa has come into the supply room or what he has taken. But it's past two thirty in the afternoon now. And according to Rosa, he should already be over at the hotel ballroom for the Teamster Union meeting starting soon. So what the hell is he doing in here?

Luis holds his breath until the cart, and Rosa, have left the room. He hears the door close, hears the click of the latch. He stays frozen until the sound of that squeaking wheel has been gone for a full minute. Then he moves forward, reaching the aisle where the cart was being loaded, eager to know what Rosa was collecting in such volume he needed a cart to carry it all.

When he comes around the corner of the aisle, he looks at the stacks of supplies, trying to figure out which inventory item has been taken. What he sees doesn't make a lot of sense. There is only one thing that comes in small cans and which appears to have been taken in any number.

Why would anyone want to take dozens and dozens of cans of Sterno, the jellied fuel that slowly burns under the tray of a buffet chafing dish to keep the food warm? He knows damn well this asshole isn't planning to serve a couple hundred pounds of macaroni at the Teamster meeting. It doesn't make a damn bit of sense to Luis.

Not yet.

Country Club, Oakmont
New Year's Eve Party

Jim is glad to see there's no line at the buffet table. He's famished, Worked up a healthy appetite shoveling snow this morning. By the time the walk and driveway were clear, lunchtime was pushed aside by the need to get all slicked up for the shindig. That's Julie—never late and often tragically early. But now Jim's mouth is watering as he approaches the steam tables and chafing dishes groaning with calories, cholesterol, and coronary peril. His stomach rumbles loud enough to make him blush.

He takes a small plate and strolls along the line of appetizers laid out. He's tempted by the mac and cheese, but it looks cold and congealed. He notices that the Sterno can under the tray has burned out, and now the food is cold.

Just as well. That crap is too fattening anyway. The real heavy entrees—like prime rib, roast turkey, broiled salmon—won't make an appearance for hours, not until the more formal sit-down dinner is served around eight tonight. That is still hours and hours away.

For now, the buffet is mostly light lunch items, snacks, and plenty of "kid food," like mac and cheese, spaghetti and meatballs, cold cuts, hot dogs, and hamburgers. Of course, there are truckloads of pastries, cookies, brownies, and ice cream. This menu is mostly for the members who bring their kids, or grandkids, for the afternoon festivities. Get the youngsters fed, sugared up, and ready to crash by around six in the evening. At that time, the younger parents will take the kiddies home and leave them with their nannies. Then the party will shift focus to the adults. They can come back and enjoy the formal dinner and dance program sans kiddos. The bar is open all afternoon, but that won't go into high gear until the party turns more "adult" this evening, once the kiddies aren't underfoot anymore, that is (and truth be told, the majority of club members, like Jim and Julie, have kids who are already off to college). But the "kids' party" is traditional holiday club highlight for everyone, even the folks who haven't brought any children, or grandchildren, more likely. Before sunset, this is a "family party"—boisterous, joyful, and bursting with wild holiday energy. This year the big hit is a really good magician who has the kiddies in awe, most of the adults too; although a fair share of them probably wish the magician would just make the kids disappear so they could really party down.

Jim just finishes piling his plate with roast beef and cheddar slices with an onion Kaiser roll. He's dying to construct a fat, delicious sandwich when he hears Julie admonish him.

"Think you need a few more cows to go with that loaf of bread and the wheel of cheese there, tubby?"

"I'm just using common sense, dear," he redirects. "Lay down a reasonable base for the excessive drinking to follow."

"Oh? Just assuming I'll be driving home, is that your plan?"

But Jim anticipates this objection and has a counter argument ready.

"Darling, my plan is to get you stinking drunk by nine p.m. and then drag you home in a taxi and start the real party."

"My objection is withdrawn. We have a lot to catch up on, seeing how much you've been gone this year."

She's only giving him the business, he can tell. But Jim is also quite aware that Julie has put up with far too much absence this year. Three big trials—all of them keeping him out of town, especially this last one, holding him down in San Francisco for nearly six months.

"I'm going to make it up to you next year, my Jewel. I mean it."

She reads his face, showing all the sincerity he can muster. She even knows he means it right now while he's saying it.

"No wonder juries love you, Jim. You could sell anything."

"Seriously, honey. I am making some changes. I know this year was tough, especially with Sarah gone too."

Julie sighs. "I didn't think it would be so…different. I mean, I get used to having you off slaying dragons, and even to missing Ellen being off at school. But once Sarah left too… I have to admit, it gets lonely."

"That's why I've hired a new… I don't know what to call her. A mentee? That's what a mentor ments, right, a mentee?"

"No, silly, a prodigy."

"Oh, that's right, my English-teacher wife."

"That sounds like you're biting off even more to me."

"No, no. Once I get her up to speed? She is going to be a huge help as far as out-of-town cases. Especially during the investigation stuff."

"Oh… *She*, is it?"

"Annette Rowan. *Mizz* Rowan, mind you."

"Ah. One of those."

"Get used to it. You can't find a female law graduate to hire who isn't 'politically correct', as they're calling it now."

"Including you own daughters," she kids, giving him a light poke in the chest with her finger. "So it's a good thing you're being trained for the New World Order."

"Maybe I should think about moving over to a civil-rights practice. Fires are going to be passé."

"Not when you're the best there is."

He looks for a trace of irony in her face but finds none. Because Julie really believes he is the best. Correctly.

"Anyway, our new *Mizz* Rowan is very promising. Stanford Law, very quick on her feet, great researcher. And the thing is, she didn't even go into law until she was almost twenty-six."

"Really? What did she do before law school?"

"Got herself a master's at MIT, no less."

"In what? Political science?"

"She is a chemical engineer. Calls herself a real lab rat."

"Huh. What made her go into the law?"

"She says it started one summer when she did some research work for a major chemical company and realized how much toxic stuff is getting churned out. She then studied the Hooker Chemical Co. (Love Canal Disaster), and that bothered the hell out of her. That did it, and most of the good chemical engineering jobs are doing *studies* for the chemical industry to show how harmless their poisons are."

"Oh, dear. A crusader. And here I was worried you were hiring a cute, young piece of fluff."

"Annette?" He laughs out loud. "God help anyone who calls her fluff."

"Ugly, then? I hope."

"I wouldn't say that. But I don't think she's very…interested in a social life. I mean, I wouldn't call her a nerd, exactly, but…she was explaining to me that there are different pathways and intermediates needed when creating a new synthetic molecule. The pharmaceutical and chemical companies always choose the easiest and cheapest pathway no matter the consequences. She's just a really serious person. That's all."

"Good. I'm glad there won't be any 'chemistry' between you."

He laughs. "Not when I have a good woman like you. A wife who loves me so much that while I go find a table to make my monster sandwich, you will head over to the bar and fetch me an ice-cold beer."

"I love you, Jim. Which is why I will get you a beer, and you will skip the ice cream after your half-a-cow sandwich. Okay?"

"Deal," he says.

Jim starts toward an empty spot at one of the tables but stops and looks back at her. *Damn. She really is the best-looking woman in this room,* he thinks to himself. As he turns back, he nearly bumps into one of the catering staff. But the young guy is nimble and skips out of his way.

"Oops. Sorry, son."

"My fault, sir."

It wasn't, but Jim gives him a friendly nod and heads for a table. The catering guy keeps going, completing his mission to replace the can of Sterno under the steam tray to keep the mac and cheese warm. He sets the damper half open, checking the Sterno's blue flame flickering under the dish to make sure it keeps burning slow and steady.

5

Milwaukee, Wisconsin
Annette Rowan's Condo

AT TWENTY-EIGHT, ANNETTE Rowan still reminds her roommate, Lindsey Heath, of that classic, nerdy, scientist type, the scholarly kind who comes off so shy at first; like that quiet girl you never notice in class until she's your lab partner. Only then do you awaken to see so much more than raw intelligence; to appreciate her subtle humor, her moving compassion, her openness not only to ideas but to feelings. Only then might you realize, despite the way she dresses to conceal it, just how incredibly good she looks.

It's still a mystery to Lindsey how they ever wound up roommates. Lindsey got the condo when her divorce from Carl was settled. When Annette, this dowdy-looking, bespectacled...well, nerd... answered her ad for a roommate, Lindsey wasn't too sure about her. Annette was new to Milwaukee, having just landed a job at some really heavyweight law firm. Lindsey knows that Annette, as a baby junior associate, isn't going to be making much money but enough to cover rent. The selling point that closes the deal for Lindsey is the grueling hours Annette will be working. After all, what could be better than a roommate you hardly ever see?

What surprises them both is how well they get along. Lindsey's bubbly personality and stunning looks have leveled her path from a popular cheerleader to a successful marketing career. She is so naturally sociable people are drawn to her, both in her work and her energetic social life.

Annette is a self-confessed grind. Back at MIT she's so immersed in chemistry she seldom comes up for air. She doesn't mind the occasional party, or even the infrequent but intense casual dalliance with some bright, horny Harvard guy. But she has zero interest in experimenting with deeper relationships. Her passion is for academic investigation. Annette is an unabashed lab rat.

Which explains how she blazes through a master's degree in theoretical chemistry. She's was beginning a doctoral program when she starts to question her future. She grows wary of her options. She sees how much her peers, and her mentors, are drawn into the cutthroat pursuit of grants.

She can see two paths ahead of her: remain an academic, constantly scrambling for funding from the commercial giants of the chemical industry; or worse, leave for the private sector, where these same giants dominate. In either case, the objective isn't "pure science." It is how to monetize knowledge. And where's the money? Most of it is focused on the development of industrial compounds that are poisoning the natural world or in mitigating the damage. And most of the so-called research, she believes, is dedicated to disproving the harmful effects the industry produced. It reminds her of the "scientists" who were employed to prove that smoking doesn't cause cancer or that global warming is a hoax.

Annette's disillusionment is accelerated by a specific catalyst. (She actually thought of it in that chemical frame of reference.) In December 1984, at the Union Carbide pesticide plant in Bhopal, India, an industrial accident exposed over five hundred thousand people to highly toxic methyl isocyanate gas. The disaster killed over fifteen thousand human beings instantly and damaged nearly two hundred thousand more with failing health and a good chance of cancer. The cause of this leak was clearly criminal negligence, but the company fought against settling with the victims and would continue to do so for years to come.

Within a month, Annette had dropped her PhD program and enrolled in law school. She was determined to apply her tremendous background in chemistry to a career in law where she could fight against the mega-corporations that were using their financial and political clout to escape responsibility for their criminally destructive practices. "If I'm not part of the solution yet," she was fond of telling people, "then I will become a corrosive solvent to destroy the problem."

Annette blows through law school in less than two years. No one ever goes through Stanford that fast, but she has an advantage. She's not just brilliant, she has a near-photographic memory.

During her last six months, Annette follows one case in particular, Melikian V. Dow Chemical. The claim is being argued in San Francisco, and so she is able to keep tabs on it. She even manages to attend a couple of days of testimony. It's not a groundbreaking case in itself, but what she wants to follow is the presentation of expert testimony, curious about what kind of scientific expertise is put into evidence and how it is presented to a jury.

The plaintiff, Gregor Melikian, is a big grape grower from Fresno. He is suing the chemical giant over toxicity and fire damages from a pesticide stored in his barn. What interests Annette most, though, is the law firm representing Melikian—Roberts, Davies, and Feller—especially the senior partner who is arguing the case against Dow, James Feller. She listens to the meticulous way he draws out the facts from the chemist. His questioning of the experts giving testimony is masterful, even illuminating. He coaxes out details in such a precise structure, clarifying for the layman jurors concepts that might otherwise challenge a chemistry major. His flawless performance fires Annette's mind with a new objective. She makes up her mind that she is going to land a job with Roberts, Davies, and Feller or die trying, which looks impossible. Annette hasn't even taken the bar exam yet, hasn't made inquiries to any of the major law firms that her fellow students are chasing after, and hasn't even responded to any of the recruiting pitches she's gotten. In fact, she won't even finish her final exams for two weeks.

But on Tuesday, December 2, 1986, she comes to the trial, determined to intercept Jim Feller as he leaves the courtroom. She has not picked this date at random. It is the two-year anniversary of the Union Carbide Bhopal chemical spill disaster.

The night before she drops off a letter for Jim at his hotel. It's partly a condensed version of her résumé, with emphasis on her background in chemistry. It's also a passionate mission statement, an aspirational essay in which she explains her commitment, her zeal to apply her own scientific investigative skills to a law practice focused on toxic chemical damages.

Now today, after listening to the day's arguments, she lies in wait to ambush him. She doesn't presume Jim has even looked at her letter; she hopes that if she can make an impression now, he'll take a look at it. So, to make sure he takes notice, she's determined to get his attention in person, introduce herself, and ask him to consider her qualifications.

She has barely said her name to him when Jim breaks out in a grin saying, "Damn. You're that chemist, aren't you?"

"Not anymore," she says. "I'm just finishing up with—"

"Stanford, isn't it?" he interrupts.

"Yes, right." A small glimmer of hope flares. He must have read it.

"You're in Jerry Walker's honor's seminar, right?"

Now it's Annette who is smiling, surprised.

"I'm…Yes. I didn't think you would have read my letter. I just—"

"I called Jerry last night. I don't know him well, but I respect the heck out of his work. He's a brilliant guy. And selective. You're very lucky to get into his class."

"Actually, he invited me to—"

"He told me. He says you have a thing about Bhopal."

"You could say that, I guess."

"So it's no accident you picked today to pitch me, is it?"

"No, it isn't."

She's very impressed he even knows today is the anniversary. How many people remember details like this?

"I'd really like to hear more about that. But right now, I'm late for a conference…" Jim pulls a business card from his jacket pocket. "Give me a call."

"I will. I…Is any time good?"

"Soon as you finish your classes. Now, go study. I don't want you to mess up your grades on my account. Jerry will think I'm poaching talent. Just keep kicking ass the way you're doing. Then we'll have a talk. Okay?"

She is trying to think up something to say, but all she can do is nod and stare at his card. By the time she looks up, he is slipping into an elevator just as the doors are closing.

"Thanks!" she yells, but the elevator is already shut.

6

Playa San Juan Resort Hotel
Ballroom Area

Wilfredo Torres is getting pissed. This whole thing is just another shit detail, but it makes him nervous. It's already very risky. He doesn't need anything more to worry about. Efrain Rosa better get his ass here, pronto, or 'Fredo Torres is just gonna lock the upper ballroom up again and forget this whole deal. He realizes he is absently jingling the huge ring of keys he totes around and stops himself. He might as well be ringing a bell. He furtively looks around, hoping nobody noticed. Nervous. He scolds himself. He knows jingling the keys makes him look even more nervous. He doesn't need to draw any attention, especially now. He can't even think up a lame excuse why he would just be hanging around idle by this door. He knows it looks suspicious.

He has already clocked all the extra security on duty today. A load of them too. A double shift, at least. They're not just here because it can get rowdy on New Year's Eve. The hotel people are nervous too. About the Teamsters. It's not like they don't expect some kind of trouble. There's always some sort of intimidation expected when contract time rolls around.

He also resents Rubén Delgado, the young punk running security now. He was some kind of MP in the service, Torres heard. *Fucking guy can't be thirty yet, and he's hired first thing to be Generalissimo of all the fucking rent-a-cops working for the hotel. Lucky prick*, he thinks.

Torres had to work his way up from the lowest janitor on the totem pole to get where he is now. Had to kiss ass with the union every step of the way too. This isn't the first bit of dirty work he's had to risk pulling off.

Torres is two years short of forty and feels every year of it. Feels the dead-end resentment over his rise from janitor to "building engineer." It takes him nineteen years, and now that he's made it, he realizes he has no more ladder to climb. He's no "engineer," and he knows it. He's still just a glorified custodian, a janitor with a bullshit title. And even that is just because the Union pushed it owing to his "seniority." Not that the Teamsters give a shit about how he does his job anyway. They just want his title to sound more impressive because they've made him shop steward. Like that's some big fucking deal anyway. Now, besides being in charge of wiping up puke and changing light bulbs, he has to get up in the face of all the other maintenance dudes. Now it's up to him to make them show up for whatever bullshit meeting the Union feels like holding. Not that they have any say in what goes on. No, his boys are mainly required so they can clean shit up for the Teamster bosses when they finish yapping at their stupid meetings, like today.

Only today he's hoping, maybe some of this "extra shit" he's doing will end up worth something to him. Ricardo Beltran himself, the president of the whole Local, knows his name now; has met with him, talked to him. Beltran knows Wilfredo Torres is a stand-up guy who can be trusted, counted on to do whatever it takes when the chips are down, like now. But only as long as fucking Efrain Rosa doesn't fuck everything up. Guy's a lazy jerkoff, that's the word in the kitchen. But Rosa sucks up to all the Union honchos, probably steals steaks and shit from the kitchen to grease the big boys. Plus, they know he's a fucking weasel who will do whatever they tell him.

Torres jumps a little as a squeaky sound cuts the air, startled, as Rosa suddenly appears, pushing a cart from the kitchen around the corner. Idiot doesn't even give a shit that the bum wheel announces him like a train whistle.

"Hey, 'Fredo," Rosa says. "How they hangin'?"

Torres ignores the greeting. He looks carefully around, making sure that nobody is in sight. He quickly pulls out the correct key from his huge ring and opens a door marked "No Admission—Maintenance Staff Only." It's a back entrance leading to a utility room for the Upper Ballroom.

"Get your *culo* inside. Quick."

Rosa takes his own sweet time, rolling the noisy cart through the utility area and into the upper ballroom. Torres is right behind him, quickly shuts the door, and locks it behind them. Once they are inside and there's no more chance of being spotted going into the ballroom, he sneers at Rosa.

"Fucker. You're late."

Rosa jerks a look at his watch. "*Vete al demonio*. You said quarter of. It's quarter of."

"It two forty-seven, *mongolo*."

"What? Two fucking minutes? What's your problem?"

"It's two minutes I'm hanging my *culo* out where somebody might see me."

"Hold your fucking water, *cabrón*."

I don't have to take shit from this guy, Torres thinks. He's a brawny man, hardened by many years of hard physical work. He has a good three inches and fifty pounds on this skinny kitchen rat. He gives Rosa a shove.

"Hey, *Que te den por culo*. Asshole!"

Rosa is furious, and only now does it occur to Torres that an alley rat like Rosa might carry a razor or a knife. *Shit, he's a fucking butcher*, Torres remembers. In fact, now that he thinks about it, he heard something about Rosa cutting some dude real bad.

But Torres is all jacked up on adrenalin and fear, and his aggression pushes him on.

"This shit is serious, *pendejo*. You understand that?"

"Fuck you, I'm here, ain't I, *zorra*? And I got the stuff."

"Anybody see you?"

"Duh. Of course not."

"Better hope not. You ever see Roberto Beltran when he's mad?"

"No."

"Damn right, no. That would be the last fucking thing you ever saw."

"Fine. I'll watch my step. Happy?"

"Let's just get this done. We gotta be ready by three."

Now that they are inside, Rosa notices the sound bleeding up from the first floor of the ballroom below them. Someone is yakking into a microphone. Neither of them can understand a word of what's being said. Union bullshit, obviously. But the speech is stirring up reactions from a crowd gathered in the lower ballroom: clapping, cheering, yelling.

"The Teamster's meeting," Rosa says.

"Really? No shit," Torres sneers.

Rosa ignores this. What he's thinking about is that his people from the kitchen better be making a good showing, or it will look bad for him, especially after he told them to get their asses to this meeting.

Torres grabs a couple of the two dozen Sterno cans from Rosa's cart.

He nods to Rosa and says, "Grab a couple of those, *cabrón*, and watch me."

Outside the upper ballroom, captain of the guards, Rubén Delgado, is leading a group of his security guards. He is stationing his men at intervals all over the property. He motions for one of them to stop.

"Here. Mateo, this is your sector. Patrol this area from the atrium to the casino doors. And keep your eyes open."

"For what, sir?"

Delgado sighs. *Mongolos on my team*, he thinks.

"For Martians."

Delgado leads the rest of his crack troops onward. Half of them are rookies. He thinks back to the Army. Maybe he should have reenlisted after all.

Delgado is just six months out of service. He joins up young, so by the time he leaves service after ten years, he's barely past thirty. He has ten years of training and experience as an MP, most of it as a supervisor. He has plenty of options to him for a civilian career. He thinks about law enforcement. But his cousin's a cop in New Jersey and hates it. Besides, he'd have to start at the bottom again if he went with police work.

He looks at private security. Your average rent-a-cop doesn't make much more than minimum wage. That's not for him. He kicks around Miami for almost a month after his separation from the Army. But then his brother-in-law down in San Juan tips him off about a job opening at the Playa San Juan Hotel—head of security, no less. The money's decent, and he knows back in Puerto Rico that kind of money goes a lot farther than it would in Miami. Plus, his mom lives down there. She misses him, and she's getting older.

What the hell, Delgado thinks. He has management skills and a track record to show he can handle organization and responsibility. He flies down for a visit home and checks out this Playa San Juan gig. And damn if he doesn't get the job. *Be careful what you wish for*, he thinks. These kids he's commanding aren't exactly Delta Force material.

Delgado stops again, near the swimming-pool area. Points to his newest hire, Romeo Cruz, a skinny kid who's almost swimming in his uniform.

"Cruz, isn't it?"

"Yeah." The kid sees how Delgado keeps eyeballing him, waiting until the kid remembers to add, "Yes, sir."

"You know how to work your radio, son?"

"Sir, yes, sir. No problem."

"You see anything looks wrong. Or odd. Anything. Call it in."

"Will do, sir."

He gestures for his herd to follow him, stopping at intervals to station the rest of them at various points around the perimeter of the ballrooms and the casino. He's already told his men about the Teamster contract running out. Maybe it won't mean anything. But the Teamsters do have a reputation. They're not above the occasional act of mayhem just to intimidate management to come to terms. In fact, a couple of city cops came by yesterday to tell him they are hearing rumors. He takes them seriously.

Delgado tells the cops he has put on a double shift on for today. He's got this, don't sweat it. He'll keep an eye out.

But he thinks back. A couple weeks ago, there's a small fire in a linen closet. He didn't think much about it at the time. An accident, maybe. Or was it a message? If so, he got it. He's on alert for trouble and plans to keep a lid on things here. Besides, even if there's no labor trouble, it is still New Year's Eve. Always a potential goat grab. So even if the Teamsters behave themselves, it won't hurt that he has all the extra men on duty to keep the drunks under control.

After setting his last guard on station, Delgado keys his communications mic, checking in with one of his security guards.

"Díaz? Advise your ten twenty?"

"West side of the tower, by the parking lot, Chief."

"Anything?"

"Nah. Nothing. How long are we supposed to keep this up?"

"You got a problem, Diaz?"

"No, sir, only... Well, it's New Year's and all. I mean, most holidays we get off a little early, is all."

"Not this year." Delgado listens, almost daring Diaz to keep bitching. When there's nothing, he smiles. He hits the key again. "And Diaz?"

"Sir?"

"I'm putting everyone in for overtime rates. The whole shift, every damn hour, for the whole day. All time and a half. Pass it around, will ya?"

"You bet...sir."

"Roger. Ten four," Delgado says, smiling.

Inside the upper ballroom, it takes Rosa and Torres less than ten minutes to get the place set up. The upper ballroom is almost never in use at this time of year. Normally, it would be completely empty during the holiday season. But now the huge room is crowded with furniture, new furniture, much of it still crated up. This includes hundreds of brand-new chairs and couches intended to replace older, worn furnishings all through the hotel. The Playa San Juan is scheduled to undergo upgrades and renovations once the holiday "high season" ends and occupancy falls. This remodel is expected to start in a few months.

This brand-new furniture is good quality. It features plush, comfortable padding. And like the padding in most new furniture available on the market at the time, these cushions are filled with a synthetic product called urethane foam. Urethane is durable, holds its shape well, and is resilient. In other words, after you sit on it, it springs back into its original shape instead of leaving an impression. Urethane is relatively cheap to produce but is as comfortable as just about any cushioning product on the market at any price. Its use is widespread.

In addition, urethane is rated as "fire resistant." That sounds really good, but there is a problem. The testing protocol that is accepted for testing materials like urethane is designed to show its best qualities. For example, if you hold an open flame up to it, the stuff does not burst into flame. Not right away, that is. In fact, it takes longer to ignite than most "natural" fibers, like cotton, that compete with urethane in the marketplace. For this reason, it is defined as "resistant" to ignition.

Resistant. But not fireproof. It may take longer for urethane to get started, but once it starts burning, look out. It will not only burn long and hot, but it will give off toxic chemical fumes that are more dangerous to human life than the fire itself. The thick black smoke generated by burning urethane contains hydrogen chloride, hydrogen cyanide, and other isocyanates. It is truly a killer.

It seems odd, but "fire resistant" urethane material is actually quite flammable; and once it's burning, it can produce a rapid, intense heat. This should not be so surprising, considering the original reason behind the development of urethane by the German chemical giant, Bayer. It's a company best known today for their widely used buffered aspirin as well as many other pharmaceutical products. But Bayer is not exclusively devoted to medicine. Their products have many applications, including industrial and military. Things that are an even bigger headache, one might say.

For example, urethane foam is not originally developed for use in furniture at all. Nor is it developed for insulation (which is another of its current popular applications). No, the original purpose for urethane's development in the 1940s is for use as a solid rocket fuel, specifically rocket fuel for the Nazi V-1 rocket bombs that rain down fire, terror, and death on London in World War Two. With such a proud provenance, it now seems ironic that this chemical product was repurposed after the Second World War to such benign peacetime uses as foam insulation and mattress padding.

Then again, Alfred Nobel didn't invent dynamite because he was looking to win the Nobel Peace Prize.

Back to the Playa San Juan Upper ballroom. Why, you might wonder, are all these chairs and couches, with their urethane foam cushions, locked up for storage inside this building in the first place? Finding the answer to this question will be one of the first targets of the intensive investigation of the incident which is about to take place.

Right now, though, Torres is showing his partner-in-crime, Efrain Rosa, what to do with all the cans of Sterno he pilfered from the kitchen pantry. They move methodically from chair to sofa to mattress, one item after another, scattered all around the furniture-stuffed room. One by one they pry open cans of Sterno and place them in position directly under various chairs and couches, distributing dozens of cans of the slow-burning fuel throughout the upper ballroom, uncapped and ready to light them up, just as if they were positioned under chafing dishes or buffet steam trays instead of furniture.

Torres checks his watch again.

He turns to Rosa and tells him, "It's almost time."

7

Casino Floor, Playa San Juan Hotel
December 31, 1986

THERE IS SOMETHING stimulating about the sound of hundreds of slot machines in full swing. To retired schoolteacher, Rose Harris, of Flint, Michigan, this continuous din isn't noise. To her ears, it's music more delightful than Beethoven's *Ode to Joy*. These are the "old-school" type of slot machines, nothing like the video screen computer games of today. These now-vintage one-armed bandits are the mechanical clockworks of back in the day. They operate as totally physical wonders, precise as a Swiss watch. They use mechanical gears and wheels that spin drums in high-speed rotation whenever the happy sucker drops in a coin and gives the handle a good yank. The reels tick as they spin, with a clacking sound like bicycle spokes with a baseball card flapping against them. The bells and whistles are literally bells and whistles, not electronic simulated sounds. The lights flash, and the symbols on the drum reels spin around and around at a blurring speed, until suddenly, one at a time, they snap to a stop. One, two, three, the symbols line up in apparently random order. (Although the real genius of these vintage machines is how highly programmable they are.) And every once in a while, the icons line up to match, resulting in a winning spin. Jackpot. The lights flash even faster and brighter as alarms clang out happy news like the ringing of a school recess bell. Shouts of joy explode from the lucky player, which sets off a chain reaction of hoots and cheers all around.

Then the best noise of all, a classic Pavlovian stimulus—the clanking cascade of metal coins hammering down into the steel trough in a shower of noisy metallic banging.

And right now this is happening to Flint's own Rose Harris. The quarter she just pumped into her slot machine (Cherry Madness, this model is called) has come up cherry-cherry-cherry. This has the old gal whooping in triumph, pumping her skinny, old arms. Her outburst quickly spreads the excitement, as strangers all around erupt in cheering for Rose, the lucky old bat who just hit a jackpot. (This outburst of fellowship is always followed quickly by bitter second thoughts all around—*It should have been mine!* But the first impulse is always, "Hooray! It's not impossible to win!")

Five hundred quarters shower loudly into the trough. Rose could be scooping them into buckets and running over to the cashier to trade them in for 125 bucks in real folding money. But she doesn't, of course. It takes her only the time to fire up a fresh Viceroy, and then she is dipping into the deep pool of quarters in her nearly overflowing trough. Awash in endorphins, Rose starts pumping coins back into the slot machine. Because that's how this game is played for Rose and millions of others. Slot junkies. They're all over the room, sucking on cigarettes, sipping free drinks, and riding the adrenalin high they can only get by feeding in the coins, eyes glued to the hypnotic whirling reels.

Past the end of Rose's aisle, blackjack dealer, Hector Martinez, cracks into a new deck. All the seats in front of him are full: Americans, Canadians, even a vacationing surgeon from Stockholm. They slap their bets for the next round on the green felt in front of them. Hector's nimble fingers start dealing out cards with practiced, professional speed. Arnie Marks of Pine Bluff, Arkansas, sees an ace drop face up in front of him. He peeks at his hole card and sees it's a king. He breaks out in a wide grin as he calls, "Blackjack!"

Thirty feet past Hector's table, busboy Edgar Morales efficiently swaps out butt-stuffed ashtrays for clean, fresh ones. The circle of gamblers packed around the craps table don't even notice him. They're too busy with their bets as dealers distribute chips on various side section areas of the table, Even, Odd, Pass, Come, and the point boxes, scattering chips all over the field. Finally, the stickman steers the dice over to the shooter to throw down the bones again. With his own chips in place, Perry Waxman of Decatur, Illinois, gives his wife a kiss on the top of her head for luck and rolls the dice.

Sofia Ocasio has a warm flush to her cheeks and a smile on her face as she quick steps back into the casino and hurries to the bar, signaling harried bartender, Jose Nuñez, that she is back on duty.

Down at the end of the busy bar, Reggie Foles is nursing a Dewar's. His eyes wander along the bar, scouting the talent. The cabbie who dropped him off at the Playa San Juan after his flight from Tulsa told Reggie this particular bar, one of two in the just casino (there's a total of six bars in this hotel), is the best spot in San Juan for finding some negotiable company. Reggie eyeballs a few women along the bar, but most of the females are either with a husband or boyfriend, and clearly none of the others are practitioners of the professional companion occupation. He fires up another Marlboro and turns to scan the rest of the casino floor, hoping.

Floor manager, Mario Guzman, completes his circuit of the casino, pleased with the smooth operation he oversees. The drinks are moving, the cards are flying, and the money is flowing steadily in. Everything is working just as it should. Of course, he reminds himself, it's not even three in the afternoon yet. There is a long, crazy New Year's Eve ahead, and it has barely gotten started. But so far, there hasn't been an angry drunk or a loudmouth, sore loser or even a surly outburst at one of his cocktail waitresses—not a single one of the thousand things that are sure to go wrong at some point. Everything is running so smoothly it gives Mario a chilly premonition of disaster, like fate is just storing up energy for a major fuck up.

Silly, he knows. He's just antsy because he hasn't got any problems to keep him busy. He finds it almost frustrating that he can't find fault with anything at all. Well, maybe the place is getting a little too hazy with cigarette smoke. But Mario has a solution for even this miniscule problem. He crosses the busy casino floor, steps through an *Employees Only* door, and into the engineering area. He moves to the bank of panels where all the controls are installed, for the lights, the air-conditioning, Muzak, and all the other background systems, discreetly out of sight. He steps up to the newest control panel just added a year ago. It's a Honeywell Series Four air handler and filtration system, designed to keep a fresh exchange of air circulating through the casino. The handler draws out smoky air and various lingering odors common to a room full of sweaty humans, blowing this exhaust out of the building and sucking in fresh, clean, filtered air from outside. Guzman tries not to use this new system too frequently, especially if it's very hot outside. Changing out the air too frequently can strain the air conditioning system. It can pull out too much of the cool but dirty air from the casino and replace it with air which is fresh but hot from outside. But today that's no problem. It is such a temperate, beautiful day, one of those December gems of perfect weather that draw so many guests to the Playa San Juan this time of year. Mario flips the filter system on, and the intake vents start to pull fresh air into the building while drafting out the stale, smoky clouds from the casino floor.

He smiles. Everything is perfect. For now.

8

Country Club, Oakmont

WITH HIS ROAST-BEEF sandwich tucked away into his relatively flat belly, Jim sips his beer and reaches his hand over to rest it on Julie's.

"Thanks," he says to her, looking into her gray-blue eyes and smiling.

"For fetching you a beer?" she says.

But she knows Jim means much more, knows that affectionate longing on Jim's face, and she loves seeing it again after all those months of him being away.

"What else can any man ask for in a mate?" he teases.

She arches a suggestive eye at him. "Whatever fancy crosses you mind, stranger."

"You do know how to challenge a man's imagination."

"Oh, it's not all that mysterious," she says. "I can read you like a book, mister. Large print. *Reader's Digest* typeface."

"Can you really?"

"You better believe it."

"So what am I thinking right now?"

"That you want to hold you wife very close and…"

"Go on." Jim smiles. "And…"

"And since what you really want will have to wait, you'll settle for dancing."

Jim stands and offers his hand. "You are truly amazing."

"Not really. You are truly transparent, sweetheart."

Holding hands like newlyweds, Jim leads Julie to the dance floor. The band won't set up for hours—not until after dinner this evening. There is a DJ on duty, though, and people on the dance floor, teens, shaking and jerking and wriggling to the sound of Iron Butterfly.

Jim and Julie exchange a look.

"Very romantic," he says.

She puts her other hand on his shoulder, face-to-face, and says, "I think we can manage."

Jim grins and puts his hand at the small of her back. Without a care, they glide out onto the dance floor, gazing into each other's eyes. They waltz smoothly through the teenage traffic, like the kids aren't even there, dancing gracefully, cheek to cheek, moving to a romantic musical number only they can hear, and deeply in love.

When *In-A-Godda-Divida* finishes playing, the DJ takes a break, and the dance floor empties. Almost.

Only the two middle-aged parents of grown college girls remain. Their bodies stay locked together, still gliding blissfully across the empty dance floor, lost in a music that is just for them alone.

9

Playa San Juan Hotel—Casino

A DOZEN EMPTY two-top cocktail tables ring the small dance floor tucked into the corner of the casino. The empty bandstand sits idle, but the couple approaching the tables from across the floor seems to be in a world of their own, which they are.

Ed and Angie Samuelson planned it this way—just the two of them. After four hours of splashing and digging sandcastles on the beach all morning, their two towhead kids, Mikey and Maggie, are totally conked out, right on schedule. Because the kids already love Idalia, their sitter, they won't wake up to find a stranger there and freak out. Ed and Angie are already enjoying their guilt-free, grown-up time together, knowing their kids probably won't even notice they're gone.

Neither one of them is very big on gambling, but the festive noise of the casino draws their curiosity. Entering, they're delighted to accept a couple of free drinks, offered by a charming cocktail waitress, even though they aren't even gambling. Angie spots the abandoned little dance floor over in a dark corner.

At first, Ed goes along only to sit at the little cocktail tables around the dance floor. It's a slightly quieter spot to sit, drink, and do a bit of people-watching. Ed once attended a convention in Las Vegas, but Angie has never even been inside a casino before.

"I can't believe people just throw away money like this," she marvels.

Ed shrugs. "I can see going to the horse races. At least there's something to watch, you know?"

"Oh, there's plenty to watch here." Angie laughs. "If you like crazy."

"I don't mind a little crazy," says Ed. He stands and sticks out his hand.

"What?" Angie asks.

"Let's dance."

"Dance? To what?"

"You can't hear the music?"

Angie cocks her head. Sure enough, barely audible under the shouts and bells, the hubbub of the casino, she can hear some bland cover tune playing in the background.

"You want to dance to elevator music?"

"I want to dance with my wife."

"That's crazy."

"Exactly. Look around. Crazy is what we're here for."

And so, like that other couple 2,119 miles away up in Oakmont, Wisconsin, these two people deeply in love are gliding across an empty dance floor, blind and deaf to everything but their affection and the simmering attraction growing between them.

While these two far-flung couples waltz in a blissful embrace, another kind of dance takes place in the Playa San Juan Hotel's lower ballroom. This dance is more carefully choreographed than the romantic tangos of our two couples, though. This is a dance with familiar routine steps, refined and practiced a thousand times. Each carefully rehearsed step leads in sequence to the next, designed to maximize the emotional involvement of the participants.

"Brothers! You all know how hard your Union leaders have worked for your welfare!" The amped-up crowd of Teamsters hotel workers packing the floor of the Lower Ballroom roars their approval. "We have only one goal. A better contract for a better life!" The man barking into the microphone, Aurelio Feliciano, is a master at stirring up a crowd. It's what he does best. "We have fought and argued and pleaded, all to gain the pay and the respect that your hard work deserves!"

Seated behind Feliciano on a folding chair, up on temporary stage before his frothing membership, is Roberto Beltran, president of Teamster Local 901. Beltran knows he is watching an artist at work. No doubt about it. He remembers how he had to go to bat for Feliciano with Jackie Presser himself, telling the president of all the International Brotherhood of Teamsters himself that this guy is a genius.

"He's a fucking Communist!" Presser had insisted.

"Actually, he's a socialist, but—"

"But nuthin'. What do we want with a fucking revolutionary? Are you nuts?"

But Presser isn't angry, Beltran knows. *He just wants me, the schmuck from the Local, to talk him into this. It's Presser's way. Argue about every decision, force you to take a stand, and then tell you go ahead, but it's your funeral. Typical fucking politician, that's Presser.* Plausible deniability. Keep everything at arm's length, let somebody else put their ass on the line, especially for the dirty work. Presser always leaves himself a way out. Not like fucking Hoffa, that's for sure, and look where that got good old Jimmy.

But Beltran is a man who knows how to get what he wants. He's a thick, pug-like figure, sly, wily, and cunning; a guy who got to the top the hard way; an alley fighter who takes no prisoners. Beltran knows his strengths, but also his own shortcomings. He's more than just muscle, but he knows that's the way the corporate suits in hotel management think of him. Fine, let ownership sell him short. That's why he has a front man like Aurelio Feliciano.

But Feliciano is more than that, and Beltran doesn't underestimate him. He knows the guy brings something special in his own right. For one thing, he's a brilliant lawyer. Say what you want, but the guy can tie up a whole room full of corporate attorneys in knots. He knows every slippery angle, every legal loophole, every way to skirt the law and keep the Local clean—legally clean, anyway.

"So what if he's a fucking Socialist?" Beltran tells himself. Even though he's a genuine Red all the way, Feliciano is also practical. He knows he ain't gonna start any revolutions. But he genuinely gets off on fucking with management. A true passion for the working man, and it shows. The membership knows he'd walk into hell for them, even the ones who think his politics are nuts.

But most of all, Aurelio Feliciano is a rock star when it comes to slinging bullshit. Besides being the Local's attorney, he's their public face, their press spokesman. He's even better at double-talking the media than he is at bamboozling the corporate suits. Guy could talk the salt out of the fucking ocean. Just look at him up there. These dumb fucks are eating out of his hand. He's talking them into going out on strike, even though there's a perfectly decent contract offer on the table.

It's genius. Playa San Juan is the perfect patsy for this year's negotiation. The new owners bought the hotel on the cheap from Sheraton because it was bleeding red ink. They've sunk a ton of dough into it already and plan to drop another fortune into a remodel. The last thing they can afford right now is a strike, which makes this the perfect time to strike.

The only problem, Beltran knows, is that Feliciano believes his own bullshit, thinks he's the working man's hero, on the side of the angels, helping these mooks stand up to their capitalist exploiters and all that shit, which is why Beltran is keeping him in the dark about what else he's planning, his own play to bring Playa San Juan to their knees. Feliciano's likes Presser that way—compartmental-ized—which is why Feliciano doesn't know what Beltran wants him to know. And this next part is Beltran's thing, the kind of move that got him where he is. Beltran is the guy in the shadows who gets shit done when talking doesn't work anymore.

He stifles a yawn and checks his Rolex. It's almost three o'clock. Time to wrap up this dog and pony show. Feliciano has done his thing to perfection. The membership is frothing. Now it's Beltran's turn. He catches Feliciano's eye and twirls his index finger, the signal to start wrapping it up.

10

Milwaukee, Wisconsin
Annette Rowan's Condo

THE DOORBELL RINGS.

"You want me to get that?" Annette calls to Lindsey, her brand-new roommate, who is still in her bathroom, getting all dolled up.

"Would you? It's Doug, and I'm already running late. Could you keep him busy for a few?"

Annette shrugs. Why not? She just moved in Lindsey's condo three days ago. She's only been in town a week since getting hired at Jim Feller's law firm. She barely knows Lindsey, so she might as well be accommodating.

"Okay, no prob," she calls back.

She marks her spot in the article she's reading (*The Structure of the Hard Segments in MDI/diol/PTMA Polyurethane Elastomers, by Blackwell, J.; Nagarajan, M. R.; Hoitink, T. B.–1981*) and goes to answer the door.

When she opens it, Brett Simon's very handsome face registers surprise at the sight of a strange woman in his girlfriend's place. Then he remembers=this must be the new roommate. He flashes the dazzling smile, which has gotten Brett through life very well so far.

"Hey, woah," he says, looking her over. "You must be…Angela, is it?"

"Annette," she corrects. "Come in."

"Annette. Of course, sorry."

He looks like a Ralph Lauren model, Annette thinks. *No, actually, more like a mannequin in the Ralph Lauren section of Nordstrom's. Only he talks.*

"So new roommate, eh? How do you like it?"

"The condo? It's very nice."

"And Lindsey?"

"She's almost ready. Sit, sit. Can I get you anything?"

He grins. "Never too early on New Year's Eve. Lindsey has some nice Rye. Over on the bar there?"

Annette walks to the wet bar as Brett sprawls on the couch, looking comfortably familiar.

"How do you want it? On the rocks?"

"Nah, neat's fine. Join me?"

"I don't want to be drunk before my date gets here."

Brett smiles. "Lindsey says you just moved her last week. You must be a fast worker, a date already."

"It's only Doug," she tells him. "We've known each other since undergrad. He's from here."

"Lucky for you. Having friends in town, I mean."

"Well…just acquaintances, really."

"But still. A date for New Year's Eve? Not bad."

She takes in the suggestive way Brett raises his eyebrows. She deflects this as she hands him his drink.

"Lindsey will be ready soon."

"Maybe," he says without conviction. "She can take an hour on her makeup just to go down and pick up the mail."

Annette doesn't want to comment. For all she knows, this is a sore point between them. She deflects again.

"I hear you're in…is it exercise machines?"

"Fitness equipment," he corrects with importance. "Only for the commercial market. All high-end, for health clubs, gyms, training facilities. Not the kind of thing regular people buy." He says this like *I'm a brain surgeon, not some country sawbones.* "You a member anywhere? Maybe you use some of my stuff."

"A member? Oh, you mean a gym? No, I don't really have time for stuff like that."

"Really? Hmm. 'Cause you look like you keep in real good shape."

Oh, brother. Flirting with the roommate while your date is getting ready, she thinks. *God's gift to women much, Narcissus?*

"So where is your Doug fella taking you?"

"We might join some friends of his at a party."

"You might? Or…"

"Or not. It's kinda loose."

That knowing leer again. "Maybe a quiet night at home, a midnight toast by the fire?"

She's had it with this creep, so she says, "I'm thinking auld lang syne and a quick blow job. Any other questions?"

Nope. Brett is too busy trying to brush the whiskey he spilled off his suit.

"Ah, here she is now," Annette says, smiling, as Lindsey breezes in.

She sees Brett trying to clean his spilled drink off the couch. "Already, Brett? I guess I'm driving again."

"I don't think he swallowed much yet." Annette smiles. "My fault. I used to tell jokes to my sister at the table, just to see her snort milk out her nose."

"Oh? I'll have to watch out for you, won't I?"

"Well, anyway," Annette sidesteps, "don't you look nice?"

Brett snaps his attention to Lindsey now. "Yeah. I mean, she's right. You look great, honey."

"And dry," adds Annette without affect.

Brett is on his feet now, stepping toward the door.

"Shall we get going?" He can't wait to get out of here.

"Sure." Lindsey puts on a smile for Annette. "Well. Happy New Year."

"Same to you guys. I hope you have a great night."

"We will. You too. Have fun with…"

"Doug," Annette offers.

"Well…don't do anything I wouldn't do," Lindsey says and winks.

"No danger of that, I'm sure. Brett? Great meeting you."

He looks uncertainly at her. "Thanks. Same here."

Annette manages to hold back her laugh until they are gone and the front door is closed.

11

Playa San Juan Hotel

ANGELIQUE ROLDÁN SCANS the men at the casino bar and notices Reggie Foles right off. He has that look, hungry but uncertain. She makes a wide circle around to come up behind him.

She gets very close before she asks, "Have you got a light?"

When he turns, startled, she knows she's right. The way this one fumbles to get a lighter out says he's a real mark. Bored, lonely, and looking for company tonight. No sooner has she taken her first drag, and he's buying her a drink.

Across the casino floor, busboy Edgar Morales sees an over-served American woman pull a pack of Newports from her purse. She doesn't notice when a ten-dollar bill gets pulled out along with it and falls on the floor.

Angelique has struck a bargain with Reggie before she finishes her drink. It's for the whole night, but he's willing to pay her price. Plus, he's not too bad-looking. She swallows the last of her margarita, looks right at him, and raises her eyebrows. He's not quite ready, though, she can tell.

"Let's have one more for the road," Reggie says. This one needs a little more courage first.

"Okay, sugar," she says to him then lowers her voice and leans in close, her lips nearly brushing his ear. "As long as the road leads back to your room."

Arnie Marks isn't just hot. He's riding the best streak of luck at the blackjack table he's ever had. But now he watches the loser two seats over bust out. The guy slams his hand down on the empty space on the table, the spot where he had a sizable stack of chips half an hour ago.

It throws Arnie. He feels a chill run through him.

Arnie's never felt anything like it before, like a premonition of doom or something. He shrugs it off and starts playing the next hand. He hits on a twelve and busts. That does it. Suddenly he feels jinxed. Arnie starts to sweep his pile of chips up, loading his sport coat pockets. He drops a ten-dollar chip in front of the dealer, a nice tip.

"Thank you, sir," says blackjack dealer, Hector Morales.

"Gonna quit while I'm ahead," Arnie says, smiling. "First time I've ever been smart enough to do that. Don't want to push my luck."

Across from the casino, in the lower ballroom, Aurelio Feliciano is really cooking now, bringing the Teamster crowd to a final peak of agitation as they start chanting, "Strike! Strike! Strike!"

Far from the stage, the chant reaches the back of the room, by the doors. Federico Vázquez, a bellhop and Union man to the core, is hollering and shaking his fist. He is so energized he appears to accidentally bump into another Teamster, Jorge Cora, who spills his drink.

"Puta madre!" Cora curses as he shoves Vázquez. *"Que te den!"* It escalates so predictably the whole argument looks staged.

Because it is...

But a reasonable-seeming guy, Kiko Cabrera, steps in to break it up. Kiko isn't just a big fella. He looks like a Coke machine with a head on it.

"Have some respect," the huge man grumbles. "This is union business. This ain't the time to start brawling, okay?"

The two of them fall timidly into line.

In the casino, Edgar the busboy sees that ten-dollar bill on the floor dropped by the woman. Now she's lighting her cigarette as she gossips with a friend. Obviously has no idea she dropped the money. Edgar moves in quietly, picks up the bill, and politely interrupts the yakking woman, returning her money. She snatches it away, giving him a suspicious look.

So much for being a nice guy.

Cocktail waitress, Sofia Ocasio, delivers a tray crowded with tequila shots to a table of high-limit poker players. She gets tipped with big, big chips while she chokes on cigar smoke.

Ed and Angie are still blissfully dancing as the band plays on.

Meanwhile, 2,119 miles to the north, a light snow begins to fall in Oakmont, Wisconsin, softly blanketing the unused golf course, piling up on the idle tennis courts.

Warm and snuggly inside the country club, Jim and Julie are still in their dreamy embrace, swaying to music only they can hear. With her head nestled against the shoulder of her beloved, Julie could almost drift off into dreams.

The loud clatter of a metal tray hitting the floor, along with breaking glass, startles her sharply. She jerks her head up. Over Jim's shoulder, she sees an acquaintance of theirs, Jerry Johnson. A nice enough guy most of the time, but he tends to imbibe too freely at large social events. Jim turns toward the commotion.

"Oh, great. Jerry again?"

"Poor Abby. I just want to die for her when he starts making a scene like this."

As a waiter tries to pick up the wreckage at his feet, Jerry's agitated conversation with his wife gets louder. She reaches for the highball glass clutched in his hand, but he jerks away from her, slopping booze on the floor and holding his drink out of her reach. Heads all around the room turn, watching without wanting to watch.

Julie feels Jim's arms drop as he steps away from her.

She puts a hand on his shoulder and pleads, "Please, Jim. Don't."

"There are kids in here, Julie. He can't just—"

"You'll just make it worse. Please."

"I can handle him."

"What? In ten rounds?"

"No rough stuff. I promise."

Before she can say more, Jim's moving in on the increasingly uncomfortable scene with Johnson and his wife. As he gets close, Jim pulls his car keys out of his pocket, jingling them vigorously to get Johnson's attention, distracting him from his angry wife.

"Hey, Jerry, aren't these your keys?"

"Wha—"

"Your car keys? I thought I saw you drop them."

"Huh? No, I don't…"

Jim can see a half-eaten slab of lasagna in front of Jerry's place at the table, so he says to him, "Yeah, you dropped them over by the buffet table." Jim shakes the keys again, distracting him again as he takes Jerry's free arm, just a friendly hand on his elbow. "Come on, we'll go take a look."

"But…you have 'em already."

"These?" Jim rattles the keys again, holding them close to Jerry's face. "No, no, these are my keys, see?"

"Hold still," Jerry mumbles, trying to focus. Jim stops shaking them as Jerry squints. "Those aren't my keys—"

"No, these are mine. You dropped yours. Over by the lasagna. Weren't you over there a minute ago?"

Jerry's brow wrinkle in concentration. "Uh. Yeah, I did get some, but I didn't take my keys out. Why would I—"

"Don't know. Just thought I saw you." Jim still has a hold of Jerry's other arm as he says, "But you can check over there." He tries to move Jerry with the gentlest suggestion of pressure, but Jerry won't budge.

"No, no, I got my keys. In my pocket."

"You sure? You better check."

Jerry nods. But to check his pocket while Jim holds his left arm, Jerry has to put his drink down on the table. As Jerry roots around in his pocket, Jim gives a tiny nod to Abby. She disappears, taking the highball glass. Jerry doesn't notice as a smile lights up his face. He pulls out his own car keys and holds them up like the prize from a Cracker Jack box.

"See? I got my keys, right here."

"You got a smoke on you?" Jim asks immediately.

"A smoke?"

"C'mon, let's step out and grab a smoke." He leans in. "Quick, before Julie sees me. She'll be all pissed if I backslide, you get me?"

"Oh, man. Do I."

"Then let's go, c'mon."

Jerry turns to pick up his drink again. It's gone. That's funny, he was sure he put it right there.

"What happened to my—"

"Forget that, get one later. Let's go light up, I'm dying here."

This time, as Jim pulls on his arm, Jerry goes along with him. As Jim leads Jerry out of the room, Julie smiles and shakes her head in admiration.

Jim steers Jerry out through a door to the patio which overlooks the golf course.

"Shit, it's cold out here," Jerry says, shivering.

"Wakes you right up, doesn't it?" Jim holds up two fingers in a universal gesture, saying, "Butt me, Doberman."

"Who's Doberman?"

"Never mind. Gimme a smoke." Calmed down now and chilled to the bone, Jerry pulls out two Marlboros, lights one for Jim, one for himself. Jim takes his smoke, makes a show of a quick puff, then just holds it at his side. He doesn't smoke. "Man, look at that snow come down," he says. "Isn't this just beautiful here? Man. Life is good, isn't it?"

Jerry takes a drag off his cigarette, relaxed now. "Yeah. I guess it is…"

"Making any New Year's resolutions this year?"

Jerry shrugs. "I don't know. Like what?"

"I don't know. Think about it. Anything you might want to change?"

Jerry takes another drag. Then he smiles as it starts to dawn on him.

"Jimmy, Jimmy, Jimmy…" He turns to Jim, studies his face. "You're a pretty fucking smart guy, aren't you?"

"I don't know. I try. Nobody's perfect, are they?"

12

Playa San Juan Hotel, 3:00 p.m.
December 31, 1986

IN THE LOWER ballroom, the chanting is loud enough to shake the walls.

"Strike! Strike! Strike!"

Beltran checks his Rolex again. Three on the dot. Time. He stands up, peering all the way across the room, to the doors at the far side. He catches the eye of the one guy who is tall enough to be seen, a head above the crowd. He gives Kiko a nod.

Kiko Cabrera, the "reasonable" big guy who broke up the fight earlier, catches the signal from Beltran and nods back.

Above them, in the upper ballroom, Torres watches a clock above the doors tick over to the top of the hour.

"It's three," he says to Rosa. "Let's do this thing."

In the Casino, Rose Harris sweeps up a big pile of quarters into a large paper bucket, the size of a popcorn tub. It's wonderfully heavy, and she smiles to herself as she heads for the cashier's cage to cash in for folding money.

On the empty dance floor, Angie is pressed against Ed's chest. But something tickles the back of her consciousness. She lifts her head and looks at her husband. She doesn't want to say anything, but...

"They're fine, Angie."

She nods and nestles against him again.

"We should try this with music someday," she murmurs.

"Why?" Ed asks and tightens his hold around her.

At the cashier's cage, there's a short line, and Rose joins it. Right behind her, Arnie Marks arrives and lines up.

"Wow. Looks like you broke the bank," he says to Rose.

"Thank you. Hit triple cherries. Good day for you?"

Arnie grins. "Best day ever."

Reggie sees Angelique put down her empty glass. He takes a gulp of his Seagram's Seven. He feels Angelique's hand find his knee.

"Almost ready?" she asks as her hand moves up his thigh.

Reggie glugs down the rest of his highball. He pulls the room key out of his pocket, raising his eyebrows.

She smiles. "Let's go get to know each other, sugar."

Blackjack dealer, Hector Martinez, cracks open another fresh deck. His nimble fingers fan the deck, then he starts to deal.

Sofia Ocasio makes another return trip to the bar. She hands Nuñez her order list and counts her tips while Jose works on the drinks order.

Floor manager, Mario Guzman, hobnobs with Pit Boss Victor Ferrer, both of them smiling, nodding…and knocking on wood because everything is running like a Swiss watch.

In the upper ballroom, Torres is on his hands and knees in front of a new chair.

"Get down and watch this," he grumbles at Rosa.

"I think I fucking know how to light a can of Sterno."

Torres looks up at Rosa, still standing, jaw set stubbornly. "Like you fucking thought you knew how to start a fire in the linen closet, *tarado?*"

"*Me cago en la madre que te parió,*" Rosa mutters under his breath. But he gets down on his hands and knees next to him as Torres takes the cap off a can of Sterno.

"Okay, first, you take off the cap…"

"Oh? Really?"

"Check the fuel. It should be soft, like butter at room temperature. Not hard like wax, okay? If it's stale, it gets hard to light that shit. So just get a fresh one."

"Fine."

"When you put the match over it, you don't have to shove it down into the goo. The vapors should catch. Just make sure it burns steady. Like this." Torres strikes a match and holds it over the open can. A little blue flame comes to life and flickers with a steady heat. "Got it?"

"Duh. Give me a pack of matches, asshole."

"You didn't bring your own matches?"

"I brought the Sterno. You didn't bring more matches?"

Torres pulls out a fresh book of matches and tosses it at Rosa too hard.

"You're the laziest fucking guy I've even met."

The two arsonists get busy, lighting cans of fuel under dozens of the chairs and couches. By the time they get the last cans lit, several of the first chairs are starting to smolder, giving off a thick, foul smoke.

"Let's get out of here." Torres unlocks the *Staff Only* door and opens it a crack to see if the coast is clear. He freezes. He sees two of the rent-a-cops lounging a dozen feet away, taking a smoke break.

"Fuck," whispers Torres as he pulls the door closed again.

"What are you doing?"

"Guards, asshole!"

The smoke from the furniture is building up. The first chair Torres lit goes from smoldering to an open flame.

"Shit! We gotta get outta here!" Rosa cries.

Torres jerks him by the collar. "Keep fucking quiet, *maricón.* You want to get us caught?" They both clam up. Behind them, they can hear fire starting to crackle, and from below a growing wave of sound.

"*strike! Strike! Strike!*"

The hollering of the Teamsters in the lower ballroom is deafening. Kiko turns to Vazquez and Cora and nods to them. They look at each other and then back at Kiko.

Vazquez clears his throat. "Now?"

"Yes, now, *imbécil,*" Kiko growls but low as a whisper, the sound lost in the din of the chanting Teamsters.

Cora looks from Vazquez to Kiko. "Isn't he supposed to make me spill my drink?"

"You fucking rehearsed this shit, *tarado*, you can't remember?"

"No, no. I remember." He looks down, ashamed. "I, uh…I was thirsty."

"What the fuck are you talking about?"

"It's all gone. I drank it. There's nothing to spill now."

Kiko stares from one to the other, trying to quell his building rage.

"Fucking *mongolos*. Why do I get all the fucking *mongolos*?"

Before they can say anything, he grabs them both and slams them together, their skulls colliding with a woody *thock!* like a pair of coconuts. Both of them buckle to their knees. A couple other guys turn to see what the problem is.

"Que pasa?" says a hotel valet.

Kiko throws a punch, smashing him in the mouth, bowling him into two outdoor service guys. They react angrily and shove the valet, who takes a swing at one of them. Kiko grabs two more guys and bulls them against a whole knot of Teamsters. In seconds the scuffle erupts into violent brawl and rolls through the tightly packed crowd like shock waves from a grenade.

Kiko smiles. "That's more like it."

He wades into the melee, mowing down his union brothers like sheaves of rye, and a riot is in full swing.

Outside the lower ballroom, Ruben Delgado hears the growing disturbance rising inside. A moment ago, he hears the chant of *"strike! Strike! Strike!"* go from loud to deafening and runs over. But now the chanting is an angry roar of rioting men.

He blows a blast on his whistle then keys his com handset and shouts, "Mayday! Mayday! Ten-ten in progress, all hands to the lower ballroom, stat!"

He's just about to pull the doors open to see what the hell the Teamsters are doing when the entrance explodes outward, glass flying as a rioting battle spills out into the courtyard.

Torrez and Rosa are coughing now, as choking black smoke rolls from the burning furniture.

"Fuck this," Torres rasps.

He unlocks the door and flings it open, not worried about a couple of rent-a-cops now. But as he slips out with Rosa, they see the rent-a-cops running off, responding to the call of the blasting police whistles and the shouts of the rioters below. Unseen, the arsonists take off, coughing, stumbling, and running like the devil was snatching at their shirttails.

Behind them, the draft of air from the door they leave open feeds oxygen into the fire, starting to rage inside the upper ballroom as a blazing inferno comes to life.

13

December 31, 1986
Milwaukie, Wisconsin

ANNETTE IS LOOKING out the living-room window. Snow is coming down pretty hard out there. She wonders about her friend, Doug, and worries over him driving in this storm. And it's New Year's Eve on top of that. There will be wall-to-wall drunks on the road.

She glances over at the big gas fireplace. Fake logs, but it would look nice anyway, and it would be cozy to warm up the room. She takes one of the foot-long specialty matches next to the key for the gas. She lights the match, holds it under the fake logs, and turns the gas key. The gas catches with a whoop and then settles into a reasonable facsimile of a cozy fire. She is about to close the grate but remembers the chimney flu. She opens it, giving a sigh of relief. Wouldn't look good to burn down the place her first week.

Maybe it's this near mishap that decides it for her. But she makes up her mind that when Doug does get here, she is going to suggest skipping that party where she won't know anyone anyway. She remembers there's a nice wedge of French Brie in the fridge and brings it out to set on the coffee table by the fire, with some crusty bread and a basket of good stone-ground wheat crackers.

She remembers Doug told her he bought a bottle of champagne to bring with them to the party. She goes over to Lindsey's bar, picks out two champagne flutes, and puts them by the softening cheese.

As Jim helps bundle Jerry Johnson into a taxi, his wife, Abby, breaks her huddle with Julie.

She starts for the cab, pausing to give Jim a grateful peck on the cheek, and simply says, "Thank you."

"Happy New Year, Abby," he says. "I think I talked some sense into him, but…"

"We'll see. I hope so." Abby gets into the taxi, and it pulls away in the falling snow. It's not even four in the afternoon yet, but the light is edging toward twilight already. He puts his arm around Julie, and they go back inside. They have to stamp snow off their shoes. "I am not going to be shoveling that driveway again already."

"Well, not tonight, anyway. You've already done your heroic act."

Jim turns to Julie and sees she is beaming at him. "See? I told you it would never go ten rounds."

"Sometimes I think you could talk anyone into anything."

"Can I talk you into heading home early?"

"What about the delicious dinner? You don't want to miss the dried-up turkey, do you? And what about the overdone roast beef?"

"No more dancing to no music."

"The band would just get in the way," she says.

"Who needs a crowded dance floor anyway?"

"I checked with the girls. I don't expect to see either one of them until tomorrow."

"I wouldn't look for them any earlier than noon in that case."

"Jim?"

"Hmm?"

She throws her arms around him, hugging him as tight as she can. "I am so happy you're finally home. This time was… It was the worst time yet. I really hope you can find a way to stay home. Most of the time, at least."

"Me too, Jewels. I'm working on it. That's why I hired the new kid."

"You think it will help?"

"We'll see. She seems to have a good head on her shoulders."

When the bell rings this time, Annette bounces right up from the couch, where she's been staring at the gas flames flickering in and out and around the fake firewood.

"Be right there!" she calls cheerfully.

When she opens the door, Doug does a bit of a double take. In fact, he is caught so far off guard he almost drops the bottle of champagne.

"Am I too early? I am, right?"

"Nope. You're fine."

"But don't you…" He is confused by what she's wearing. He should have left the champagne in the car, he thinks, but he doesn't know a thing about champagne, so he wanted to ask Annette if it looks any good. But all he can think about now is how she looks, which is, well, good, all right, just…not what he expected. "I mean, if you need to change, it's okay. Take your time."

"I already changed," she says cheerfully.

And she has. She has replaced the Stanford sweatshirt and mismatched jogging pants she had been wearing when Lindsey and Brett left. Now she's wearing some red-and-white-striped leggings that remind Doug of candy canes and a very long, very tight pink sweater that ends about three inches above her knees. And that's all, as far as he can tell. Certainly, she isn't the same old brainy intellect that he is so fond off.

"Don't just stand there, come in. I won't bite you. Unless you beg."

He manages a laugh on the chance she is kidding. She has to be kidding, right?

"Okay. I better take off my shoes then. They're kinda snowy."

"Sure. Take them off. That's a good start."

"Huh?"

"The champagne, I mean. Let me take it."

She grabs the bottle and carries it over to the couch by the fire, where she already has an ice bucket.

"That was going to be… I mean, I thought we'd bring that to the party."

She watches as he fumbles to untie his wet shoelaces. "You obviously see how terrible the weather is out there. I really don't feel comfortable driving anywhere tonight."

"Oh. Really?"

"Doesn't a cozy night by the fire sound good?"

He grins, walking over to the couch. "Honestly? That sounds great."

"I think so," Annette says. "A perfect New Year's Eve." She tears a hunk of crusty bread off the loaf. "Sit down," she insists. "Right there."

He sits on the couch next to her.

She has spread Brie on the bread and says to him, "Open."

"What?"

"Your mouth? Open."

He opens, allowing her to place the morsel on his tongue. He really enjoys eating it.

"Wow. That's good."

"Do me."

"Oh, okay. Sure."

Doug prepares a little piece of bread, spreading the cheese on; and as he turns to her, she opens her mouth wide and closes her eyes. He has a little hitch while he fights the impulse to kiss her. But he puts the treat on her tongue, and she chews it, eyes still closed.

"Mm." The way she moans makes him want to kiss her even more now. She swallows and opens her eyes. "Let's pop it open. Shall we?"

"Heck yeah," he says, pulling the champagne from the ice bucket and uncorking it with a loud pop that fires the cork across the room and sends them both into giggles. He pours two glasses and lifts one to her. As she clinks her glass with his, he says, "Happy New Year."

She smiles a coy smile, lifts the flute to her lips, and downs it in one long slug. And then she lowers her eyes and begins to quietly sing.

"Should auld acquaintance be forgot,
And never brought to mind…"

Doug downs his own glass in one gulp and joins her singing.

"Should auld acquaintance be forgot,
And days of auld lang syne…"

They stop singing.

Her eyes roam over him, and he starts to reach out for her, but she says, "Doug…" and leaves it hanging.

"What?"

14

Playa San Juan Hotel
The New Year's Eve Fire

IT IS NOW a little after three in the afternoon of December 31, 1986, at the Playa San Juan Hotel in San Juan, Puerto Rico. There are several hundred guests packed into the casino. Across from the Casino, over a hundred Teamsters have just turned their union strike vote meeting into a riot. Inside the twenty-story tower, the hotel guest rooms are all rented; although many guests are out of their rooms and starting to celebrate the New Year's Eve holiday.

And in the upper ballroom, two arsonists, looking to create chaos and put pressure on the hotel management to cave in to Teamster Hotel Workers Local 901, have just started a fire.

Chief of security, Rubén Delgado, is trying to marshal his vastly outnumbered forces to put down the rioting Teamsters spilling out from the lower ballroom. Nightsticks flail. Fists are thrown. Bones break.

Delgado thinks his New Year's has gone to hell.

But as he punches and shoves and wrestles with the rioting Teamster hotel workers, a sharp, stinging sensation causes him to wrinkle his nose. Smoke? Not just plain smoke but an acrid, chemical smell, almost like a whiff of tear gas.

He turns his attention from the melee for just a second, glancing up the broad staircase which leads from ground level to the upper ballroom and the atrium entrance to the hotel. Most of the time, you can't really see into the ballroom from the outside. The wall is mostly floor-to-ceiling windows, which have heavy drapes to keep out the heat of the tropical sun. But today the heat is inside the ballroom. And little by little you actually can see inside—because those curtains are on fire.

A shrieking blast on his whistle as Delgado screams, "Fire!" into his coms microphone. He starts grabbing his guards to rally. The rioters, too, lose interest in fighting, as everyone out here can see clouds of black smoke roiling out from under the ballroom doors at the top of the stairs.

Delgado dashes for the steps to the upper ballroom. After climbing just a few stairs, his lungs are already burning. The higher he climbs, the worse it gets. He's a relatively young man, just a few years past thirty. He's in decent shape, not all that different than he was during his ten years in the Army. But his legs falter. He struggles to keep going, a chemical stink is searing his throat. His legs give out, he falls to his knees. He fights to get back up and keeps going…

Inside the casino, riding a decent buzz and with a hot-looking hooker on his arm, Reggie Foles is feeling pretty damn good as they head for the exit. Angelique Roldán notices the smell just before he does. She stops, her hand suddenly gripping his arm. Now he notices too. They freeze just short of the door, checked by the sharp stink. What is it?

Busboy Edgar Morales notices the acrid smell. This is not the usual smoky foulness he expects as he empties ashtrays. It's different. It's bad.

Angie and Ed go still on the dance floor as she begins to cough. "I smell smoke," Ed says. Then he, too, is coughing.

Mario Guzman's first instinct is to look up at the vents of the air-conditioning and circulation system. Why is there a smell? He has those new air scrubbers running. They should be cleaning the air, but it's getting worse instead. Something isn't right.

Rose Harris finally reaches the front spot in line. She is next. Behind her, Arnie Marks taps her shoulder, points to the now-vacant cashier window, where clerk Duldin Valentín is beckoning to her. But suddenly Rose is wheezing. Arnie catches her as she staggers,

74

dropping her big bucket, and hundreds of quarters hit the floor and scatter in every direction.

Out on the steps to the upper ballroom, Delgado manages to stagger halfway up the stairs. But he is wheezing, fighting for breath. Now his youngest recruit, Orland Diaz, trots past him. Even though the rookie is in perfect condition, he has to stop just short of the upper-ballroom doors, gasping at the pain in his throat. He fights through a spasm of gagging coughs and somehow struggles up the final steps to the landing above. He is only six feet from the upper ballroom doors when the fireball explodes through the glass, a thousand razor-sharp shards shredding young Diaz like slaw.

And now the dragon is loose.

A whole wall of ballroom windows blows apart, and the surge of fresh air lets the roaring fire grow almost instantly from conflagration to an explosive inferno. Fed by the huge fuel supply of urethane cushions (thank you, Bayer, for the German solid rocket fuel), a blazing ball of superheated flame flashes across the atrium between the ballroom and the casino.

Angelique grabs Reggie's arm, trying to turn him back, away from the door. Too late. The blast of flame blows apart the casino doors as flaming chunks of burning urethane, superheated gas, and deadly smoke roils into the packed casino, roasting everything and everyone in its path.

The panic begins.

Flames spread rapidly through the casino, igniting the papered walls and moving across the crowded floor. Screams of pain erupt, and cries of fear roll across the casino, as deafening as the roaring flames. But while the uproar of sound from the fire grows louder, the screams can't keep up. The voices of human agony are choked off by the billowing clouds of poisonous chemical smoke.

Mario Guzman realizes his wonderful new vent system, ironically intended to clear the room of cigarette smoke, is only sucking more fresh air into the burning room, feeding oxygen to the fire like a bellows. He attempts a futile dash across the casino floor to reach the control panel. He never even gets close.

By now every soul in the casino is scrambling in blind, choking panic. The stampede of terrified tourists quickly becomes a mob of trampling, desperate lunatics, driven mad as a devil's tidal wave of flaming death presses in on them.

Arnie Marks tries to lift Rose to her feet, but she swoons into a final blackout. He drops her, tries to flee, but is bowled over by dozens of fear-crazed tourists and staff. He convulses with violent coughs as he tries to stumble back to his feet. But he is repeatedly knocked down hard, kicked, stomped, and trodden over. The over-stuffed pockets of his sport coat tear open, but nobody thinks about trying to pick up the thousands of dollars in casino chips scattering across the bloody floor.

In the cashier's cage, clerk Duldin Valentín pulls a special alarm, locking down the money room. He is locked behind bars, safe from the trampling herd. But his priorities are all wrong. As the black waves of toxic smoke overcome him, he realizes his attempt to save the money is his death warrant.

Blinded by the smoke, Ed desperately calls for his wife, Angie, barely rasp from his burning larynx. He trips and falls on top of a body. Her body, Angie's chest crushed, her legs and neck broken by hundreds of feet that thundered over her in terrified flight. Ed tries to scream in his grief-stricken horror, but all he can do is hack and cough. He tries to lift her body, he staggers a few steps, and then he drops, blacking out as the toxic gases fill his lungs.

From behind his bar, Jose Nuñez waves frantically for Sofia to shelter with him so she isn't trampled. Bruised, clothing torn from the stampede, she fights to get closer and finally squeezes behind the bar for shelter from the crushing mob. But Jose and Sofia are coughing, hacking up toxic smoke as it darkens the room in spite of the brightly roaring flames. Then a blast of superheated air flashes across the rows of bottles behind them. The glass all shatters, dumping hundreds of liters of alcohol, showering down, soaking them. Seconds later, their shaken bodies perish as the vapor of the volatile spirits bursts into flame.

The victims mount as the fire spreads. Those few who manage to escape the broiling flames, or avoid being trampled to death, find their lungs burned by the toxic clouds of hydrogen cyanide. Fumes of caustic isocyanates fill the air, burning their skin, blinding them and choking off their air supply. The tendrils of smoke curl around them like the grasping fingers of Death, seizing them, stopping them in their tracks, crushing out life after life.

Some gamblers manage to reach exit doors by the far wall, which would open to the beach. This might offer a last slim hope of escape. Only these doors have been locked. In fact, they are chained shut.

There are still a few other exits, far in the back, which are not locked. But these doors have a fatal design flaw. They are hung to open inward instead of swinging outward. So as the panicky crowds surge against them, the bodies so desperate to get out, press themselves against these doors, pushing the wrong way. The force of the surging mass behind them crushes them harder against the doors. The press of human panic makes it impossible to open the exit doors, blocked by the very people trying to escape. It is a crushing horror as the flames and toxic smoke claim more souls.

These deathtrap doors are not the only built-in fault in the hotel's physical structure. As the expanding fire and deadly smoke extends to include the main hotel, with its twenty-story tower of guest rooms, the path of destruction should be interrupted by a fire sprinkler system. And the building's smoke alarms should be triggered, blasting out shrill sirens to warn the guests in their hotel rooms of impending danger.

Only there are no sprinklers. There are no smoke alarms. There are no fire codes or regulations in place to require them. In fact, despite the expensive and grandiose designs for the soon-to-begin remodel of the hotel, there are no plans to add them. The intended remodel does not include any safety upgrades. Not that any future plans would matter now. All that counts in this cataclysmic moment is that the guests in the fire's path have no warning at all, not until it is too late.

By the time babysitter, Idalia Romero, realizes the oncoming threat, there is little she can do. She wakes the precious children Ed and Angie entrusted to her care, hysterical herself as the terrified children. They rush from the room, only to see a curtain of flames down at the end of the hall. They dash for the elevator, but it has broken down. Through the rapidly growing fumes, they choke and stagger, stumbling desperately, trying to reach the emergency stairwell at the far end of the hall. The toxic smoke kills the two youngsters first. And as they drop at her feet, dying, Idalia collapses to her knees with a desperate, choking wail. Her will to escape dies with them, and she surrenders her soul to the smoke's fatal darkness.

A handful of guests manage to cheat death, leaping from windows, crawling through the few available exit points, or dragged to safety by brave, determined staff or security guards. Tears stream from Rubén Delgado's soot-streaked eyes as he screams himself hoarse, directing his men and pleading for help over his radio. His own security people do all they can, but where are the emergency responders?

They are coming. They are coming as fast as the traffic-clogged streets of San Juan allow. But every road within a mile is glued down with traffic, bad enough when it is not a holiday, let alone with boozy drivers awash in rum to celebrate the coming of a new year. Police abandon their cars in a struggle to clear a path for fire trucks. All of them are stuck, unable to bring aid. They can only stare helpless at the terrible vision of that column of deadly black smoke rising like a gigantic tombstone just a few blocks ahead. It is almost an hour later when the first firefighters reach the scene.

The only help that arrives before them comes by air. News helicopters swoop to the scene, intending to train their cameras on the holocaust unfolding below them. Then they see them—a handful of desperate hotel guests who have somehow reached the roof come into view. There is nowhere to land on the roof, of course. But one by one the brave pilots hover as close as they dare, each managing to airlift a handful of guests who manage to reach the skids and scramble aboard. It is a sight not unlike those desperate attempts to pluck the last survivors from the roof of the American embassy as Saigon fell. Only these news copters are not large military choppers built to carry squads of soldiers. These compact little helicopters are only built to handle three people at maximum load, including the pilot. By twos and threes, they evacuate those few they can, hovering close, buffeted by the dangerous swirling updrafts of the raging fire below, then struggling to stay aloft, dangerously overloaded by the lucky few who can make it aboard.

The fires burn out of control for hours. Over time, survivors are located, many suffering terrible burns from the flames. Many more whose lungs have been damaged for life from the deadly chemical smoke. Some of the toxins will hide like time bombs inside them, patiently waiting to generate chronic illness or eventual cancers—a death toll that keeps on giving.

At the time the fire starts, the hotel is operating on a skeleton staff, of course. This thin crew is due to so many of the hotel's on shift employees being temporarily absent, attending the meeting of their Teamster Local. To their credit, once the fire explodes from the upper ballroom, many of these hotel workers stop the riot they had started and do all they can to assist in the largely futile efforts to save the guests and their fellow staffers. But driven back by the heat and the killing clouds of deadly toxic smoke, there is little anyone can do. Death is loose on a wild rampage, drunk with a lust for destruction, and this is his day to take the field.

Two other men emerge from the lower ballroom as their rioting membership leave. The sickening realization of what he put in motion slaps him in the face, and Ricardo Beltran's color drains.

"Holy bleeding mother of Christ," he mumbles. "*Me cago en Dios*, what the fucking fuck did they—" But he cuts himself off as the sly animal inside him reawakens, and his feral instinct for self-preservation kicks back in. He shuts his mouth.

His second-in-command, Aurelio Feliciano, feels his own guts twist in a normal human response to the unfolding horror before him. He doesn't know anything about how this fire actually started. His initial shock is only due to the staggering human toll before him.

But when he hears Beltran's voice and the way his boss suddenly clams up again, something inside Feliciano tells him there is much more to this.

He turns hotly to Beltran, trying to read his face, and asks, "What were you saying?"

"Nothing. Just, I mean, look at this, for God's sake. Jesus."

"I see it," Feliciano says coldly. "Tell me we had nothing to do with this."

"Fuck are you talking about?" sputters Beltran, puffing up rage to meet this insinuation. "*Me cago en tu puta madre—*"

Feliciano's hand shoots out, grabbing Beltran's arm, squeezing down on the bicep as hard as he can. Beltran is shocked at the man's strength. This lawyer, this civilized man of letters, has never touched him, certainly not with such potential for violence. Hell, not one of the most brutish Teamster thugs in his local would dare lay hands on Beltran. Nobody would, not in thirty years anyway. But when he sees the coldblooded look in this lawyer's eyes, Beltran knows this moment holds so much in the balance.

"I am asking you only once." Feliciano's frosted tone is as serious as the deadness in his eyes. "I need you to say it to me."

"Say? What are you—"

"Say it plainly and directly when I ask you. Because I will ask only once, and I will act on what you say. I will take your words for the truth. I am bound by oath to my professional duty. And I will do my job. What that duty is depends on what you tell me right now. Did we have anything to do with starting this fire?"

Beltran understands. He has to tell his attorney what the man needs to hear, not what he doesn't need to know and doesn't want to know.

"I swear on my mother. I don't know anything about this, you hear me? Nothing. *Nada. Nada!*"

And it is done.

They both know Beltran is lying. But for Feliciano, his client has answered him. He can honestly say under oath, if it comes to that, he has asked, and that is the answer Beltran gave him. He will never ask Beltran again.

He nods once, turns, and walks away from this monstrous horror. He keeps moving. He must keep going because he knows what must surely lie ahead. He will have to be strong. He will have to advocate for his client.

But for now, he cannot allow Beltran to see the tears running down his cheeks. He allows himself this one moment of humanity, only now, only once. Then he must put it away and do his job.

Beltran keeps staring at the raging inferno before him, unable to look away. It is so loud, he thinks, much louder than he'd have imagined. The roar of the inferno pushes against him, a wind of its own. As loud as a jet engine, he thinks, as the terrible noise washes over him. But not so loud he can't hear the screams.

When he notices someone beside him, Beltran turns sharply. Kiko Cabrera stands by his side. He looks at his boss, not the fire, waiting.

"Find those two *pendejos*," Beltran orders. "Bring them to me."

PART TWO

THE PARTY'S OVER

15

Oakmont, Wisconsin
New Year's Day 1987

FOR A NEW Year's Day, Jim thinks, waking up at nine twenty is pretty darn early, but not so early that Julie is still in bed. She's gone, which dashes his first waking thought, which is to reach for her. But no, she's up and about already. Either that, or the bacon he smells is cooking itself. Still, it's bacon, almost as pleasant as his first waking impulse, which was to grab his wife. He is consoled with the pleasant memory of their private New Year's Eve celebration. You could say their ritual of getting reacquainted was greatly satisfying to all parties concerned. A symphony of intimate renewal was played in several movements, a concerto lasting well past midnight. *No wonder I never even think about wandering*, Jim thinks. *Why bother? I've already got a woman who can never be topped.*

A shower is tempting. But it's no match for the irresistible smell of bacon. Jim slips into the pajamas he never did end up wearing last night and lopes down the stairs.

Julie's back is to him as he leans in the kitchen door. The sight of her in a big, drab, dowdy apron makes him chuckle because Julie is wearing it to protect the racy peek-a-boo baby doll she put on display last night, lingerie which is an inspiration to the monkey business that followed.

"Scrambled eggs," she calls over her shoulder, sensing him without needing to look. "Your choice on potatoes. Home fries or hash browns? Haven't started either one yet."

"We have onions to fry with that?"

"Yup. So hash browns?"

"Right. What's that you're listening to?" he asks about the stream of a mellow announcer's voice, burbling from the old clock radio in the corner.

"Nothing. Just WBBM."

"All news, all the time," he teases. "What's the big headline? *'Baby of the Year born one twenty seven a.m. in Hammond, Indiana*?"

"For your information, it was a girl, in Council Bluffs, Iowa, at just seven minutes past midnight."

"Guess I lost the office pool."

"Good. Your damn office is the last place we need to think about today. Any games on yet?"

"I don't know. Maybe the Cold Cereal Bowl or whatever. I swear, they must add three new bowl games every year. I can't keep up anymore."

"What time is the Rose Bowl?"

"Who cares. I hate Michigan."

"Such a sore loser. What was our record again this year?"

"Wisconsin? Hmm. I forgot."

"Three and eight," Julie rattles off. "And if I'm not mistaken, we lost a real squeaker to Michigan. Forty-nine to nothing, was it?"

"I hope you get bitten by a badger, you disloyal, old harpy."

"Go turn on the TV set. See if there are any games on yet. I'll let you know when the grub's ready."

Reaching around her, Jim endures a sharp rap on the back of his hand with a spatula, a small price to pay for the slice of perfect crisp of bacon he steals on his way to the den.

He flips across all four channels they get out of Milwaukee, plus the snowy ghost of NBC's Chicago affiliate, which comes in and out sometimes. He finds some stupid parades, a rerun of some sitcom he vaguely remembers from the seventies. No games yet. As he shuts off the TV, a garble of words from the news radio station in the kitchen reaches him.

"The fire ignited the furniture (garble, garble)...out of control, growing to massive proportions and..."

Jim's ears perk up. He heads back toward the kitchen, picking up the broadcast more clearly as it continues.

"After flashing over from the ballroom, the superheated gasses swept up the grand staircase into the lobby of the hotel..."

"Where is this?" he asks Julie, who just shrugs.

"I wasn't listening. Puerto Rico, I think?"

"The fire was sucked into the open doors of the casino by the smoke-eater ventilation system present throughout the casino..."

"Shh, listen..." Jim hushes her. He soaks in the newscast, eyes narrowing.

"Most of the deaths occurred in the casino, as guests discovered emergency exit doors were locked. The only other egress from the casino was a pair of inward-opening doors..."

Jim closes his eyes, shaking his head as the tragic details continue to unfold. Julie turns to him. The news is awful, but it is the grim look on Jim's face that hits her in the pit of her stomach.

"Casino patrons pressed against the doors to no avail. Some guests leapt from the second-story casino through plate-glass windows to the concrete pool deck below..."

"Jim? This doesn't mean you'll have to—"

Julie doesn't even get the rest of her fateful question out when the phone hanging on the kitchen wall starts to ring. She wants to step into his path, to block him, but Jim is already moving to answer it. His stomach goes cold as he picks up the receiver.

When he learns who is calling him, Jim notes the bitter irony of listening to WBBM, the CBS news radio from Chicago, while at the same time he is fielding a call from CBS Television News Headquarters in New York. He doesn't know the name Don Prescott. But the secretary putting his call through tells him that Prescott is a producer for Dan Rather, the CBS Nightly News anchor and star of *Sixty Minutes*, their top-rated Sunday show. Prescott wonders if Jim can be available for an interview.

"I don't know anything about this fire," Jim says. "I just this second heard about it over the radio, and—"

"That's okay," the news producer assures him. "Nobody knows much of anything yet. It's just breaking."

"Well, there you go then. I don't see how I can help."

"Jim, you're too modest. I doubt there's anyone in the country who knows more about hotel fires and toxic smoke. We have reporters for the fire details. But Dan wants to talk to someone with your perspective, who can explain deadly chemicals and fire damages so a layman can understand things, and well...Dan asked for you."

"Who? Dan Rather?"

"You're the best expert we could hope for. Nobody else has your reputation when it comes to explaining these things so even a dope like me can understand."

"I don't know...Don, is it? I just got back from a long trial."

"Understood, I get it completely. We're not talking about today. Just want to see if you can be available, maybe late tomorrow? I'd set it up with a reporter who could come to you. Do it right at home. Or wherever you want. I'll get somebody from our network affiliate in Chicago to go up there."

Jim looks over at Julie and reads the anxiety in her face.

He covers the receiver so he can say to her, "Easy, Jewel. It isn't work. Some guy wants me to talk to Dan Rather."

"Just talk? That's all?"

"A quick interview. Smoke, toxic chemicals. I'm sure it won't take long."

"Today?"

"No, no. Don't worry about that. Maybe tomorrow. Who knows, by tomorrow there might be a bigger story someplace, and they'll chase after that instead."

Jim realizes that Don Prescott is still gabbling away at him even though Jim has the phone covered and isn't listening. He lifts the receiver back to his ear, trying to pick up the thread.

"...of the victims didn't die from the flames, as much as all the smoke from the burning stuff, what's it called? I had it right here...

Ah. Urethane. I guess that's what most of the furniture was made of, or whatever."

"Urethane foam. They use it for padding inside the cushions."

"Yeah. That's the thing. That's what they set on fire."

Jim perks up. "Set? Someone set the fire? Deliberately?"

"Right. Looks like it was arson. So between all that stuff about burning chemical materials and the fact it's a hotel? You've done a lot of work with arson fires like this, right? You'd be perfect to explain to our viewers what the authorities will be looking for, you know. How stuff like this gets investigated and all that."

"Yes, but I don't know. I'm not so sure I want to go on TV. That's not my thing."

"You don't need to decide now. First, let me see who I can find to go up there from Chicago. Meanwhile, you can just think it over. I'll call you back this afternoon. You can decide then, okay?"

"Maybe. We'll see." He holds his look with Julie, her eyes brimming insecurity. "I need to talk it over. My family, you know? We have plans, and… Just call me later." Jim hangs up the phone.

Julie is still half listening to the radio news report. She looks utterly appalled at what's coming over the air now.

"What?" Jim says. "It's pretty bad? Huh?"

Julie switches off the radio. "They say over a hundred people are dead, Jim. The worst hotel fire ever…"

"Did you hear anything about how it started? This CBS guy says it looks like it could be arson."

First game on is the Cotton Bowl. Or is it the Sugar Bowl. Jim can't seem to get very interested in the little figures racing around on his TV screen. It's an early kickoff, not even lunchtime yet. But there's a ham and cheese on rye Julie made for him, sitting untouched on a tray, right next to a bottle of Pabst Blue Ribbon, growing warmer and flatter. He is slouched in his favorite chair in the den. But Jim Feller's mind isn't here. It's more than a thousand miles away and half a mile below the surface of the rocky Idaho ground.

Jim tries to chase the ghosts back, to get free of them and leave them where they belong, deep inside the shafts of the Sunshine silver mine. It's not a big town, Kellogg, Idaho. Almost every person there knows more than one of the miners down there in that death-trap hole. It takes days and days of searching to find all the bodies, slow going, with pockets of deadly gas still lingering. Twenty bodies, thirty, forty. Men sweat and struggle, miserable in gas masks and thick protective gear. The cavernous mines run for miles and miles, shafts and tunnels branching in every direction. Fifty, sixty, seventy. They just keep finding them, more and more bodies, twisted and horrible, in twos or threes; corpses who died in terror and agony, trapped in mine shafts that were overheated sweatboxes even during a normal work shift. The dead men ran every which way, in ever more futile desperation, trying to find a safe corner in the endless hell, running until they stumbled, crawling until they dropped, through the endless labyrinth of tunnels carved out inch by inch by their own labors, dug out by strong, proud miners over decades of drilling and blasting, clawing treasure from the richest silver mine in the world; men who died in choking darkness scattered through tunnels in dozens of different levels; men who toiled through pain and terrible hardship to earn a living for their families; men who spent their lives literally digging their own graves. Eighty dead. Ninety dead…

The last two men weren't found until day nine of the search. They were all the way down on level fifty-four, over a mile below the surface. And when the search party finally reached these last two miners, the thing that shocked the whole world most of all was this…

These two men were still alive.

The jangling ring of the phone jars Jim out of his memories. For a moment, he has to look around, reorient. The den. TV. The phone. It must be noon now, he figures, judging by how the edge of his sandwich is a bit curled and looking stale.

He grabs his lukewarm bottle of Pabst as he crosses the den to pick up the extension from the side table by the bookcase, expecting it will be that CBS guy again. Jim doesn't think he can stand to so much as think about another fire right now, especially not one as horrible as this hotel thing sounds, more especially if it was arson. Besides, who could give a damn about listening to him blab away with Dan Rather anyway? Nobody wants to hear some lawyer yak about how much money this disaster will cost somebody. The only thing anybody watching TV wants to hear about is how many people died. They don't need Jim for that.

Talking to fifty million viewers about a fire like this is the last thing Jim wants do. Nobody could make them really understand the horror of such a fire. And the fact is, they wouldn't want to know. Once you get something like that in your head, you can never stop knowing it. It's always with you, deep inside, a tiny ember that can roar back into a monstrous nightmare anytime it gets loose in your mind again, which you can't stop from happening, no matter how much you want to.

The phone is still hammering away.

He takes a swig of the warm beer then lifts the receiver.

"Jim Feller."

But it's not CBS, not this time.

"Happy New Year, Jimbo."

Jim knows the caller's voice at once, a voice which has grown very familiar over the years. Ronald Cunningham is senior partner at Ramsey, Cunningham, Raskoff, and Greenberg. It's a firm that corporate money sloshes through in massive tidal flows. Very few businesses in Los Angeles can rival these oceans of cash, except maybe the movie studios. Ramsey, Cunningham is a firm you approach only if you are very, very rich and in very, very deep shit.

"Same to you, Ron. And no."

"Jimmy, Jimmy. You don't even know what I'm calling abou—"

"Puerto Rico. Right?"

"This thing is right in your wheelhouse, Jim. And I need you."

"Then you can watch *Sixty Minutes*. Dan Rather wants to interview me."

"No, no. Don't do that. Very bad idea."

"About that, I agree. I don't want to do it anyway." He takes another nip at his tepid bottle of Pabst.

"Good, good. Now listen, we—"

"Ron, don't waste your valuable, billable hours on me about this. I want nothing to do with another one of these...mass casualty things. Seriously, I don't think I could stand that again."

Ron Cunningham listens, taking that in. He can hear the pain in Jim's voice, knows the horrors Jim has seen: hotel fires; burned factories; mines and farms and even schools; terrible fires that have killed so many in such terrible ways; death from flames, from smoke, from toxic poisons. He understands. These horrors can drive any man to the edge of despair. He knows Jim has seen more of them than any man should have to bear.

Ron feels awful for poor Jim Feller.

"Jim, I understand. If I were a half-decent human being, I'd just hang up and call in the next man up."

"Good," Jim says. "Have a nice year."

But he doesn't hang up because that's the point. It's not over. Ronald Cunningham is many things, but a half-decent man? Not on the list. Not even close.

"Tell me," Ron says, coming in sideways, "how much do you know?"

"More than I want to."

"Over a hundred dead already. They're still counting."

"Terrible, Ron. I know how that must be tearing you apart. Just think of the damages. A real fortune at stake here, I'd say."

"Okay, fine. I'm a cold bastard. But I have a duty to be practical about this, Jim. The cost will be astronomical. It could destroy my clients."

"Who do you represent? No, don't tell me. The bastards who sell that poisonous urethane crap, right?"

"Jim, if you'd listen—"

"They deserve what they get. They know how bad that stuff is, and they just keep using it because nobody stops them."

"You're right," Ron concedes. "Assholes. Can't agree more. I wouldn't touch them."

Jim almost laughs. If Ron Cunningham wouldn't touch them, it's only because he knows their case is a certain loser.

"So? Who then?"

"We're representing the hotel."

"Ha! Good luck with that."

"Now listen, Jim. I admit we have huge exposure here, no question. We're going to take a big hit, no way around that. But we don't deserve to eat the whole thing. That just isn't right. It's not the hotel's fault if the manufacturer put that poisonous crap in the cushions."

"That's not going to be much help, and you know it."

"Ah, but we have other mitigating circumstances."

"What? Argue that the poor hotel didn't know urethane smoke is toxic? Bullshit. The plaintiffs can show how it's killed people in a hundred fires already. Good luck with that defense."

"The point is, this fire wasn't the hotel's fault. Did you know that?"

"I heard it might be arson. Hard to prove, I bet."

"Not with this one."

"Why's that?"

"Because my client was directly targeted by a criminal enterprise."

"Who? Business rivals? Blame it on Motel 6?"

"Very funny."

"Who else, then? Drug cartels? Democrats?"

"Try the International Brotherhood of Teamsters." Ron gives it a beat. "Remember them, Jim? Remember Las Vegas?"

The MGM fire: sixty-five dead, suspicious origin, no proof who did it, no witnesses—none that lived anyway. That fire was right around contract time for the Teamsters with the hotel. Nobody could prove the link. But Jim knows.

Two years later, a huge electronics distribution warehouse in Toledo was having problems negotiating a contract for their drivers. The problems ended when the whole place burned to the ground. Only six dead that time, but nearly a thousand men out of work. Again, nobody could prove who started that fire. Although most of them knew—the Teamsters.

"Ron. The last thing I want is to watch those bastards walk free again. I swear to God, it kills me to think about it."

"That's why you can't say no to this, Jim. This is arson, a slam dunk."

"All those fires were arson. Pinning the arson on the Teamsters? That's something else."

"Not this time."

"Sure, right…"

"No, really. There's a ton of physical evidence this time."

"What about witnesses? Anyone who will swear they did it?"

Jim notes a hitch of hesitation before Ron says, "I know one thing for sure, Jim. If anyone can dig up a witness to testify against the Teamsters, it's you."

"If there's anyone to stop witnesses from talking, it's the Teamsters."

"This is different. There are a lot of dead hotel workers. Those people were Teamsters too. They've killed their own people. Folks who have friends. Families. Other Teamsters, with firsthand knowledge of what happened and motivation to talk."

Jim almost believes him. But this is Ron Cunningham, a man who knows how to be convincing, however not exactly a man whose word you take at face value. Besides, even if Ron is right, this won't work for Jim. Right now there's no way he can turn around and leave Julie again for who knows how long. No. Not even for a shot to finally nail the Teamsters. It's not right.

"Jimmy?" Ron says, not liking this silence. "Just go down there. Take a look. That's all I ask. Don't take my word for it. Go see for yourself."

"I'll have to think about it."

"Don't think too long. I can't wait around. This is too hot. I have to get somebody on it while the evidence is still fresh."

"I know. I said I'll think about it. I'll let you know."

"Today. It has to be—"

"Later, okay? Stop pushing."

"Sure, sure, I understand. It's bad fucking luck though."

"What is?"

"Well, if you do this job, you'll have to blow off Dan Rather."

Jim doesn't give a good damn about Dan Rather, or Ron Cunningham, for that matter. What worries him is Julie. Until last night, he had no idea how vulnerable she is feeling. Of course, it's no surprise she misses him when he's gone. He misses Julie just as much.

Hell, the last six months in San Francisco he felt like he was missing an arm.

But last night, after all their dancing and the fun and the love-making… It all felt so good, so right. Then in the dead of night he finds Julie awake, crying. Jim's been asleep for an hour. Then, what with all the champagne and everything, his bladder wakes him up. That's when he hears her—no, he actually feels it first. The way Julie is shaking as she sobs, he can literally feel the mattress shake. She is faced away from him, her weeping almost silent, but he can feel her tremble. He reaches for her. His touch makes her jump.

"Jewel?" he says softly. "What's wrong, sweetie?"

"Shh. I'm sorry. Go back to sleep."

She stifles her crying, going stiff with the effort. But he moves closer, arms enfolding her, pressing against her body. He can still feel the tremors she is trying to hold back.

"It's all going to be okay, Jewel. I promise."

"Oh, I know. I'm just being silly. I'm so happy you're back."

"I am back," he says, meaning it. "I know how hard it's been."

"I thought I'd be better this time. Get used to it, you know? By now? But…it's just, the house feels so empty. You'll see. With the girls gone, I mean. You'll see how much you miss them, what I'm going through."

"It will be fine, baby. You'll see. I'm back now. We'll get used to it together."

"I know, I know." She turns over now, facing him. She burrows her head against him as he holds her. "I love you so much."

"I love you, my Jewel."

That was last night. Now he has to talk to her, has to go to her, let her know he won't do this thing, won't run out on her when she needs him most. He knows he can't avoid it. He has to tell her, really mean it, so she can believe him. They'll talk through it together. She will give him the strength to blow off Ron Cunningham and Dan Rather and everyone else. The two of them will spend the rest of the week with the girls, maybe drive down to Chicago for a day, the whole family, all of them together right up until the moment the girls have to go back to school. Then it will be just them, the two of them, like it was in the beginning. Everyone else in the world can just go to hell.

He finds Julie in the kitchen again. That damn news radio is still nattering along. He catches something about a death toll in San Juan now reaching 110. He walks straight over to that old clock radio and switches it off.

"Why are you even listening to that?"

She shakes her head and shrugs, can't seem to find words.

Then finally, she says, "I heard you talking. Ron Cunningham?"

"Did you hear the part where I told him no?"

"What I heard on the radio…they're saying it was Teamsters."

"I don't care."

He notices, as he says this, how she won't look at him, afraid to read what she fears she will see in his face.

"Don't say that," she says. "Of course, you care. I know that."

"I'm sick and tired of chasing those bastards. Let someone else go after them. Really, I don't want any part of them, not again."

She turns to him. "I know you don't want to. I believe you. But you can't say no to this. You can't. Not after Las Vegas."

"Jewels. That's…look, it wasn't easy, but I had to put that behind me. And I have. I've made my peace with it."

"I know you've tried. I've seen what it's cost you. But this time…" She shakes her head. "Even on the radio, it sounds pretty obvious they did this. And it's just like them too."

"Proving it is something else. As we know."

"I know what it will do to you if you pass this up."

"I'll get over it."

"Stop lying to yourself. It would stay with you, Jim, the rest of your life. You'd regret it every day."

"Jewels. That's just not true."

"Isn't it? Look at me." She stops closer, right in his face. "Look me in the eye and tell me this is something you can just walk away from, that you can do that and not look back." She stares at him hard.

"I can, Jewel. I will." And he does mean it, or he wants to mean it. He really, really wants to mean it. He can't leave her again, he can't, not now. "There's no way I can take this on. I can't do that to you."

"No!" She's angry because she knows him. "You can't make this about me. I won't have it. Do you think I want to live with that? Knowing I'm the reason you throw away your one chance to finally nail those bastards?"

"I would never think tha—"

"You would and so would I. Every time you look at me, that's what I'll see. The regret. It's in your eyes already, Jim. I can see it."

He reaches for her, but she steps away. She doesn't want to be comforted. She wants it out, all of it, out in the open—the truth—for the sake of the rest of their lives together.

"If you don't take them on now? The rest of my life, I'll know why. Because of me. I don't think I could stand that. I won't. I can't."

"No. Jewels, really. You mean so much more to me than getting into all that madness again."

"I love you, Jim. As a husband, a father…as the only man I've ever wanted to be with. But I love *you*. All of you, the man you are. I will not be the person who stops you from doing what you know is right. Because, damn it, Jim, that's who you are. Like it or not, that's you."

"But Jewel. I just can't—"

She stops him with a finger over his lips, steps in close to him, hugs him desperately. "You have to take this case, Jim. You know it, and so do I."

They are still standing in the kitchen, locked in an embrace, when the phone rings again. It's CBS calling. Jim tells Don Prescott he can't do that interview, Dan Rather or not. He has a duty of confidentiality to his client.

As soon as he hangs up from the CBS call, Jim is dialing Ron Cunningham. In his mind, Jim has an obscene amount of money he will ask for. And Ron is going to pay it. He has other demands, all kinds of unreasonable conciliations he will insist on. He will get everything he asks for. It will be Jim's show, all of it. He will do everything exactly as he sees fit, and nobody will be able to get in his way.

He'll have his own people, all of them, and as many as he wants. He will have every resource he decides he needs, period.

It's going to cost Ron Cunningham a boatload to get the best. And that is what Jim is—the best.

16

Milwaukee
Annette's Bedroom

SHE'S ASLEEP, HER face lying on Doug's chest. He's on his back, so he snores a little. But a little snoring is not going to keep Annette awake. They are both too exhausted. Long night. Lots of exercise. It's already past noon, but they've only been asleep for a few hours.

The shrill buzz of her pager has Annette bolting upright and jumping up. She dashes, naked, to grab the pager off her dresser and shut it off. She shivers a bit, as the cold January air raises goosebumps on her whole body—a surprising body, lush and toned and full of springy life, one hell of a lot better looking than you might expect, considering how stogy she looks in her usual wardrobe.

When she sees the number she is supposed to call back, Annette forces herself wide awake, even if she is still a touch tipsy and on the road to hungover.

"Oh my god!" She says it louder than she means to.

This forces Doug to open one eye, a painful squint at the cruel daylight intruding into his life. He watches Annette grab the Princess phone on her nightstand and punch in the number she reads off her pager.

Doug gets all whiney. "Aww, c'mon. What're you doing?"

"Shut up, Doug. This is work."

"Work? It's New Year's Day."

She ignores him as her call goes through to a busy signal. She slams the phone down. Oh Doug, she has known him forever, it seems. She admired his brilliant, scientific mind. They are such good friends and date on special occasions when they need a romantic sexual encounter (like last night), but love never enters the picture. Now it is back to reality.

"I gotta shower and get ready to go."

"But it's New Year's. You shouldn't have to work."

Annette lets the water run to get hot while she steps back into the bedroom. He's still lying on his back.

"Doug. Get lost now. I'm serious, I have to get ready for work."

"How do you know? It was busy."

"Why else would I get a call from my boss?"

"To say Happy New Year?"

"Just get your stuff and get out, okay?" She starts back into the bathroom. "Sorry, Doug. And thanks. It was great. But I really have to get going."

Annette returns to the bathroom, not even bothering to shut the door.

As Doug hears the shower curtain slide shut, he yells, "I'll call you next week?"

17

Trans World Airlines Flight 1639
31,000 Feet Above Bowling Green, Kentucky

JIM FELLER CHECKS again. The first class seat behind him is still empty. He didn't see anyone in it before when he and Annette board the plane at Chicago O'Hare International. But he just wants to be sure. He tilts his seat back as far as it goes, hopes he can grab a power nap. A glance over at his young associate, Annette has a fat brief-case open on the floor in front of her seat, brimming with briefs, abstracts, letters, contact lists, scientific data, maps, summaries, etc., and judging by the weight of it, when Jim offers to put in the over-head bin, several lead plates. But Annette stops him; she doesn't want it put up anyway. She shuffles one document after another, in and out, working with singular concentration. As it appears to Jim, she always does.

Before takeoff, Annette admits she's never flown first class before. But the posh setting doesn't appear to matter much to her, Other than leg room she shows no interest in any of the perks, gour-met-taste treats, or free booze. What she does appreciate is the slightly larger fold-down seat tray which allows her to work more efficiently.

Earlier, leaving Milwaukee on a chauffeured ride to O'Hare air-port, she informs Jim she's never ridden in a limousine either. The reason they are taking this ride, Jim tells her, isn't for the luxury. There are no direct flights from Milwaukee to Puerto Rico. They could fly down to Chicago then change to a connecting flight, but doing it that way not only takes longer; it carries the added risk of lost luggage, or even missing connections. Plus, if you consider travel time to the Milwaukee airport, parking, checking in luggage, getting aboard the plane, then getting off again in Chicago? It all takes around three hours at best, if there are no delays. But their eighty-six-mile limo ride will take less than ninety minutes and get them directly to their terminal at O'Hare, door to door from home without the stress of scrambling.

If Jim thinks the time they save will give him a few moments to get to know his industrious new associate any better, it turns out there's little chance of that. Skipping the chitchat, Annette takes the opportunity to directly grill him for details about how to approach their investigation and the case as a whole. She demonstrates a savvy focus beyond her years and impresses Jim by the way she draws him out on things the average associate wouldn't even think of asking in the first place: the politics of dealing with Ron Cunningham and his LA firm, the attorney-client relationship with the fractious consortium who owns the hotel, the need to interact with local Puerto Rican authorities, and especially how to deal with the tangle of federal agencies they will have to navigate through the investigation. There's the FBI, the ATF, OSHA, and the whole alphabet soup of other organizations, agencies, and departments layered into the federal bureaucracy. She soaks it all up like a sponge and probes for deeper details in all the right places. He finds himself taking unexpected delight in the way she asks all the right questions and her ability to draws excellent conclusions.

Jim realizes he must have dozed off when he is gently awakened by a flight attendant. She's offering a small, hot towel to clean his hands and wipe his face before they serve the meal. She confirms he requested the filet.

"And it's the salmon for you, ma'am, is that right?"

"Sure, whatever," says Annette.

Jim turns to see she has put away her mountain of documents. Now she's buried behind today's newspaper. Earlier, Jim remembers, he grabbed a copy just before they boarded the plane. But he's never had time to get a look at it. The paper is dated January 2, 1987, and the front page is light on hard news. It's largely the scores of all the big bowl games from New Year's Day. But the hotel fire is there too, on the front page, but below the fold. As the stewardess moves on, Annette lowers the paper and smiles.

"Nice nap?"

"I'm still making up for New Year's Eve. Barely slept." He stretches as much as possible in the confines of an airline seat. "Julie and I—she's my wife—we had a…" He stops, a smile at the memory. "Let's say, it was a festive night. But then all of yesterday I was scrambling to line up this trip. Up half the night, too, with this and that. By the time I got to bed, I couldn't sleep."

"I didn't either. I was too excited."

"You're twenty-what? Twenty-eight?"

"Twenty-nine next month."

"See? You won't even need to sleep until you're thirty-five."

"Good to know."

"Unless you have little kids. Then you never get to sleep, period."

"I'll make a note of that too."

"So…before I sprung this goat grab on you, I hope you at least had a nice New Year's Eve."

"I did. Just a quiet evening at home with a friend."

"Huh. My girls? Both still in college. Anyway, they didn't even get home until midafternoon yesterday."

"They must have had a good time too, then."

"I know better than to ask what they were up to. Besides, I couldn't keep them home unless I locked them in their rooms."

"I know what you mean." She offers Jim his newspaper.

"You done with it?" he asks. "You're welcome to finish reading—"

"Oh, I have plenty to keep me busy."

And she dives back into her huge attaché. Jim takes to the newspaper and starts to read about the fire.

Teamsters Local Spokesman Denies Any Union
Connection with Blaze with Hotel Fire
EDWARD L. PAQUIN, January 2, 1987
SAN JUAN, Puerto Rico (AP) Teamsters
Union officials issued a press release today, stat-

ing they did not direct members to take violent action against the Playa San Juan Hotel and do not condone the fire on New Year's Eve that killed ninety-six people. The statement was issued by spokesman, Aurelio Feliciano, a longtime attorney on behalf of Teamster Local 901 president, Roberto Beltran.

"The Teamsters did not advise, incite, nor induce any of its affiliated workers to set the hotel on fire nor to commit any crime at the hotel," the union's statement proclaims.

Attention has focused on the union in part due to a labor dispute with Playa San Juan over a new contract for hotel workers. Talks on a new contract for the union's 250 hotel employees broke down, and the union planned a strike to begin January 1, 1987. Preliminary investigations suggest the fire may have been deliberately set. A spokesman for Playa San Juan Hotel suggested that hostile labor-management relations at the hotel might have been a criminal motive.

Cont. page 9

18

San Juan, Puerto Rico
Headquarters: Teamsters Local 901

AN IMMACULATE, SHINY, late-model Cadillac convertible squeals to a stop by the front door of a nondescript commercial building housing Teamster headquarters. The stop is so sudden it rocks the powder-blue vehicle on its springs. Roberto Beltran throws open the driver's door so hard it bounces back on the hinges and hits him on the shin as he leaps out. He is already purple with barely suppressed rage, and the painful whack on his leg blasts him right off the batshit meter.

Screaming a nonstop torrent of *shit-fuck-puta-cunting-mierda-me-cago-tu-puta-madre-cocksucking-motherfucker*, Beltran slams the driver's door shut so hard the car rocks and begins to kick dents into the pristine, perfectly buffed side of his own car, scuffing his hand-stitched loafers. His frenzy is so violent he soon finds himself gasping, out of breath.

As Beltran stands panting, a burly Teamster cautiously steps out the building's entry doors. Pablo Cortez looks like a pro wrestler gone too fat, and his scarred face and flattened nose do not suggest a fearful man. But as he creeps warily toward the caddy, Cortez keeps his eyes aimed down at the asphalt. It's the look of a whipped dog. He practically cringes as Beltran, still puffing out obscenities, scuttles past him and goes inside. Pablo sighs with relief as he walks over to Beltran's ragtop Caddy. It's still running, key in it. Pablo's familiar pattern, whenever Beltran arrives, is to take the boss's car and park it. This time, before he gets into the driver's seat, he pauses in his usual pattern, to regard the brand-new auto's battered door panel. *Christ. Beltran kicked the shit out of this*, he muses. *His own fucking car.* Once again, the sheer brutality of this man's temper makes an impression on Cortez. Then he gets in behind the wheel and, as usual, drives the boss's car off to his reserved parking slot.

Beltran steams past the front desk, ignores a welcome from the receptionist, and plows through the pool of front office staffers without slowing down. Office workers scramble like ants when lifting a rock, throwing themselves out of his path. Nobody is fool enough to meet Beltran's fury-crazed eyes.

He blasts through a door at the rear of the open plan office and storms into the utility area in back. He makes a beeline across the supply room, heading for an office at the back. Without even slowing as he passes by, Beltran grabs a mop from a bucket, knocking it over, spilling gray sludge across the floor. He doesn't care. Still barreling forward, he snaps the wooden mop handle in half with his bare hands like it's a matchstick. He flips the wet mop head end away with a careless toss. He grips the remaining busted end of the mop handle like a billy club.

Inside the back office, the two arsonists, Efrain Rosa and Wilfredo Torres, stand trembling. A black eye here, a bruise there, visible clues that their escort, Kiko, wasn't so gentle when he collected the two men and brought them here. As they tremble, Kiko looms behind them, impassive, his thick arms folded.

Beltran rockets in through the office door, already screaming, "Fuckheads! What the *fuck* did you do?" He is swinging his improvised cudgel as soon as he gets close enough, filling the air with crunching smacks. *"¡Me cago en la madre que te parió!"* Their whimpers and excuses don't slow the boss down. *"¡Me cago en tus muertos!"* The men try to absorb the furious blows, but in seconds they're both beaten to the floor. Bleeding, pleading, they lie curled and helpless at Beltran's feet, screaming in pain, trying to avoid letting the club strike anything too vital. *"¡Que te folle un pez!"* Beltran beats on them with a metronomic rain of blows, regular and methodic strikes, each blow accompanied by a single exploding profanity.

"You. Stupid. Fucking. Morons. Do. You. Know. What. You. Mother. Fucking. Assholes. Did? You. Fucked. Every. Man. In. This. Union."

Beltran tries to land a kidney kick or two, but that doesn't work out for him. His foot is still throbbing too painfully from kicking his own car, which only fuels his anger as he goes back to work with his makeshift club, hammering at them with the regular, efficient pace of a woodchopper splitting kindling.

19

Ruins—Playa San Juan Hotel
January 2, 1987

VALARIA MARCOS WAITS at the airport in San Juan to meet the plane delivering Jim Feller and his associate. She knows Feller by reputation only, but if anyone can prevent the total financial devastation of the hotel's owners, they all say Feller is the one. Valaria is the legal liaison to Playa San Juan Hotel's cantankerous consortium of owners. They are a precarious alliance of jealous competing interests, temperamental personalities, and not-so-silent partners who make a lot of destabilizing noise. The group is vacillating, volatile, and capricious. What could go wrong?

Ordinarily, Valaria is hardly the choice for such menial duties as meeting planes to chauffer people around. Errands like this are far, far below her pay grade. But right now, there is too much at stake, and she needs Jim to hit the ground running.

Valeria's own climb from *humble beginnings* (or what we in the States might call abject, Dickensian poverty) reveals what a remarkable woman she is: too exceptional to be denied and never willing to accept defeat, refusing to listen to all those negative voices telling her to forget about attending college, disregarding the dismissive chorus who assume her entering law school is just a ploy to find a good match and get married. Again and again, Valaria defies the macho mafia of resistance in a male-dominated business world. Her success is all her own, her rise the result of indomitable will, and her undeniable excellence allows nothing to hold her back. She is a trailblazing, cage-rattling, glass-ceiling-busting woman who can't be denied.

Valeria smiles to herself, remembering how she lays it out to Ron Cunningham. *Either get me Jim Feller for this case, or I fire your useless, fancy-pants law firm.* And somehow, Ron does it. Here's Feller, complete with protégé. Now she hopes it was the right call. Better be.

Valeria turns to Jim and offers to have the driver swing by the Hilton and get them booked in.

"Forget that. A waste of daylight. Take us right to the scene. Then the driver can swing back to the Hilton and drop off our bags."

"You sure you don't want to freshen up first?" She looks from Jim over to Annette, who has her face buried in some document.

But without looking up, Annette is obviously paying attention when she says, "We didn't come down here to raid the minibar and take a dip in the pool," she mutters, never looking up. "Let's get to work."

Valeria smiles to herself. Something tells her she picked the right team.

As they step out of the car at the site of the Playa San Juan, Jim hears Annette give a barely audible gasp. He knows it's more than just the visual shock at the devastation left behind by the fire. It will take many hours to take in the overwhelming scale of that destruction. But the first thing to hit them when they step out of the cool, sealed comfort of an air-conditioned Lincoln are the smells.

There is the expected and unmistakable char of burnt wood, of course. But that's only the first layer, a base, the foundation. Then you notice how the air still carries a sharpness. This acrid sting of chemicals is an alarming smell, one that screams an automatic warning in the brain. *This is poison. This will kill you. This is very bad stuff.*

But these first terrible smells are not the stink that makes your flesh crawl. A stronger odor assaults you, fouler than all the rest, more visceral. This is what really knocks you back, a gut punch of a smell, one that immediately starts the gorge rising in the back of your throat.

It is death—a smell that is here from the very start while the fire is still burning. The first layer of death's stench is the immediate sickening wave of burnt hair and overcooked meat. But that first putrid stink hasn't really matured yet. But by now, almost forty-eight hours since the blaze began, the worst of death's terrible reek is starting to overwhelm all the rest, the mounting decay of dead flesh accelerated by the humid, tropical heat. This stench hits you hard, makes you want to step back.

Even if you have never come across the smell of death before, you'd still recognize what it is, what it means. You can't help it. It's built into your DNA, a survival instinct. The flashing lights on nature's ambulance, a shrill insistent siren, this unmistakable warning, all screaming whistles and clanging bells—it grabs your attention and won't let go. This smell draws an unambiguous line in the sand. It is the Reaper's own calling card, and it slams you with the most existential warning there is. This message is literally a matter of life and death.

Jim tries to read Annette's face. How this first moment affects her might make all the difference in the world. This assault is so powerful it can stop the strongest man in his tracks.

It takes only a moment for her to process where she is and what lies ahead for them. This isn't about law or chemistry or even money. Before any of that, she realizes, the path before her leads right to that most fundamental of truths—death.

She turns to Jim. "Let's get our cameras and gear up, Boss. Like you said, we're wasting daylight."

20

San Juan Hilton Hotel
January 2, 1987

ANNETTE AND JIM order a second bottle of wine.

Before dinner, almost as soon as they were checked in, they hit the cocktail lounge. Silver-haired bartender, Antonio "Call Me Tony" Nogueras, has been at this a long time. He's the kind of professional bartender who knows when a customer needs him to be a little freer in his pouring, and these two just have that look. They've been through that kind of day. They're three drinks deep when Tony suggests it might be a good idea for them to think about heading for the dining room.

Jim nods, helps Annette down from her barstool, and leaves a pair of twenties on the bar for good old Call-Me-Tony.

It really was that kind of day.

There are tents set up when they arrive at the fire site. They change into coveralls, heavy-duty work boots, orange vests. Safety gear is issued: hard hats, protective gloves, N-95 filter masks, goggles. Practically sealed head to foot, their personal protective gear roasts them like an oven. Sweat pours, goggles fog constantly, and dehydration hovers like an evil spirit.

Before they can even approach the wreckage, they must have several inoculations: tetanus boosters, tropical vaccines, a panel of prophylactic medical precautions. They are introduced to field scientists from the FTC, CDC, EPA, ATF, and a battery of Puerto Rican law enforcement and security groups. Annette starts the first of many geek sessions about air samples, surface samples, autopsy procedures, and toxicology reports, going over mountains of technical requirements. But this chatter is cut short, to be continued. Jim waves her over to meet another investigator.

Mike Peralta looks like he could be the model on the cover of an FBI recruiting pamphlet, steel-gray eyes that sweep the surroundings like perimeter sentries or stop and drill into you with intense focus. The set of his jaw conveys both determination and devastating good looks. He has full, expressive lips that take on an almost-pursed expression when he is listening to answers, along with a tiny tilt to his muscular neck which gives him a quizzical appearance of focus and concentration. Despite his overalls, which cover him head to foot, it is easy to discern that the man inside has a large, powerfully built body. Later, when she finally gets a look at Mike in street clothes, Annette takes a tiny bit of pleasure to see he is dressed exactly as she had pictured he would be, a drab, durable dark suit—conservative tailoring that is both classic and totally dull. The choice of tie around his thick neck always looks out of place, something he only wears as a concession to convention. They're invariably boring, solid colors, sturdy and impervious to style. Whatever they are made of, it's always a material far more washable than silk, for sure. His no-nonsense white shirts have a far-too-unwrinkled look which scream "no iron" fabric; shirts with not a whisper of cotton or any other inconvenient natural fiber. His shoes are solid practical foot coverings, standard boring design. Even his socks are boring.

But there is one feature that distinguishes Mike's footwear. The soles—not the usual leather sole, the kind that gives little traction. While the uppers are standard, the rubber soles have the appearance of running shoes, complete with ripples and ridges, built for traction; shoes that can help a man when he has to run fast. Pursuit shoes.

Peralta gives each of them a business card, pointing out an office number, an answering service number, a pager number, and even a home number.

"Not that you'll necessarily need to get hold of me on short notice. But just in case…"

Jim can read the serious look on Mike's face. "You're working the criminal end of this, I assume."

"If there is one," he says, lawyerly and noncommittal, then the wink and frankness. "So far? It sure looks that way."

"You wouldn't be with any kind of organized crime task force, would you?"

"No…at least not formally." With a look implying yes, he says, "I know damn well who we are dealing with here. I did take the trouble to glance over your résumé. So I don't have to tell you to watch yourselves, dealing with Teamsters."

"I take it you're pretty satisfied that this was arson."

"It was set deliberately. No question about that."

This turn in the conversation stimulates Annette's technical interest. "Was there any accelerant found?"

"Let's put it this way," he says, warming to her sudden show of interest. "There's nothing accidental about somebody scattering two dozen cans of Sterno all around a room full of furniture then lighting them all at once. That was our point of origin."

She turns to Jim. "Maybe we can start by taking a look there?"

"We will. Sterno or not, we always start where the fire starts and follow wherever it takes us."

Their plan is to walk the path the fire takes. Jim works as methodically as any chemistry professor she's known. They move along at a good clip because the idea for this first pass is to get an overall sense of how the fire moved and how the destruction spread. So they don't bog down in details. Not yet.

Their cameras are never still as they both churn through roll after roll of film. They don't divide up the scope of their photo sweep. Both cover every angle, which might seem redundant, but Jim's theory is that doing it this way gives them a wider perspective. Even if two people photograph the same thing, they will never frame it exactly the same way. There will always be a slightly different view, giving a different set of information. Not only that but when you look at a photo you've taken yourself, you have already seen your own angle. So the brain tends to see what you expect because you "know" what you've seen the first time. You might glance right past something you missed. But looking at photos taken by someone else can force you to concentrate, looking closer for these little differences. It's like the kid's game; one of these things is not like the other.

Their objective today is to document as much of an overview as possible while it is still "fresh." Every minute that goes by changes that condition. The other people swarming over the fire site have their own particular and specific fields of interest, but Jim and Annette are trying to get a generalist's picture first. So from the upper ballroom, they keep moving, following the path the fire took as it expanded.

While everyone working the scene tries to preserve the conditions, things change rapidly. The first priority when the ruins cool enough is to start inspecting the recovery of the dead, to determine the human cost. Even before Jim arrives, bodies are being recovered and stored for later evaluation. As this grim harvest moves forward, the number of victims mounts. Many bodies are so badly burned identification will be difficult. In a way, though, these totally charred corpses are easier to look at. They are so thoroughly altered you can almost forget this thing you are looking at was once a living human being.

But many of the dead haven't been burned that much at all. Annette finds these corpses are even more horrible to view, if possible, because what killed them wasn't the consuming destruction of the flames. So many victims were killed by the choking toxic smoke. They still have a face, and their frozen expressions offer grim confirmation of the terror and pain, the utter panic when there is nothing to breath but searing poison, That moment when death becomes a certainty.

Annette is surprised by this difference between the crisply burned corpses and the relatively intact dead, but Jim is not. Today's tortured dead find plenty of company inside his skull. They join the legion of souls who have taken up residence in his mind, so many fire victims who have checked in but will never check out: miners trapped under Idaho's rocky ground; farmers trapped in burning livestock barns; factories, hotels, theaters, and schools; even churches; victims who never expect life to be ripped from them when they enter a large hog-feeding structure or a huge commercial chicken coop. Often the fire itself can look so minor, a small blaze burning in a limited area. But the fire's fuel is what kills them, unseen urethane insulation or harmless-looking furniture cushions. But as these materials burn, cyanide lies in wait for them.

The victims here at the Playa San Juan join the vast ranks that haunt Jim's dreams. There, in his head, these new ghosts join a special place reserved for the victims of other hotel fires. These latest initiates to Jim's mental morgue find company with seventy-six gamblers from the MGM Las Vegas fire whose luck ran out. Their fate was delivered not by the turn of a card or even the fatal random hand of some fatal accident. These ghosts owe their deaths to a labor dispute which led to arson.

Not that it matters to these innocent victims. Teamsters or no Teamsters, they are just as dead.

The fire's raging march to mass fatalities leads out from the upper ballroom, crosses the open atrium, and blasts in through the doors of the crowded casino. Here death has come in many forms: killed by fire, by superheated air, by toxic gases, and choking black smoke.

But perhaps the hardest deaths of all are those souls who didn't die directly from these perils. They are the people who died at the hands of their fellow victims, or more accurately, died at their feet, crushed, broken, trampled to death; dozens of lives stamped out under the heels of other panicked gamblers desperate to claw their way out of the deathtrap casino. This is the most sickening twist on the massive slaughter. It hits Jim and Annette in a way that feels somehow even more tragic. It also angers them to find so many killed just as they reach their last shred of hope, crushed in reach of their only chance to escape, killed right at exit doors that would not open, either by negligent design failure or worse, because they were chained shut. Somehow, this seems to be the cruelest fate of all.

But there is also a special sorrow reserved for those helpless, innocent people who die inside the hotel hallways, victims who didn't die in the full swing of celebration in the casino. These were guests minding their own business, thinking themselves safe inside the comfort of their resort hotel room, like the two little children found dead, sprawled on the floor with their babysitter. They have paid the worst price, dying in complete innocence.

A waiter comes by, asking Jim if he is still working on his barely eaten steak.

"Go ahead, take it. I'm done."

Done with the food anyway, he thinks. He pours another glass of wine from their second bottle. Annette nods, yes, she will too. They both sit, processing the day's horrors in separate silences.

"It's bothering me," he says.

"Of course, it is. It's so awful. So many people…"

"I don't mean the bodies."

"No?" She waits. Then she has to ask, "What then?"

"Those goddamn doors. Somebody chained them shut."

"Who do you think it was?" Jim says nothing, not meeting her eyes as she presses him, "The Teamsters? Is that what you think?"

He stares at the wine in his glass, shakes his head. "I don't know. It could be, but…I don't think so. That makes no sense."

"Well, who else could it be?"

He shakes his head again, sadly. "That's what bothers me."

She wrinkles her brow. She doesn't quite follow him. Maybe her brain is just to fried from exhaustion, and wine. She runs her hand over her face, yawns, stands up, and wobbles a bit.

"Whoa. That's it for me." She picks up her half-full wineglass and dumps it into the ice bucket next to the table. "Good night, Boss. Meet you here for breakfast?

He stares for another beat then brings himself back. "Huh? Yeah, eight o'clock. See you then."

"Okay. Good night." She starts to turn away.

"Annette?"

She stops and turns back to him.

"Yeah?"

"Today… Out there. You did well. It was tough to look at, but you did well. I appreciate it."

"It was bad. But…not as bad as I thought. It was…not 'interesting,' that's not the right word for it, but…provocative, maybe? So many questions, I guess. Such a challenge. I don't know, it sounds kinda harsh when I say it out loud, but…that's just me. I always need to find answers."

He looks up at her.

After a moment, he nods. "So do I."

The moment sits, feeling heavy, then she turns again, saying, "Anyway, I think I'll take another shower before I go to bed." She smiles and heads off.

Jim watches her leave the dining room.

"You do that, kid," he says quietly. "But it won't wash off that easily…"

21

San Juan Hilton Hotel
January 3, 1987

IT IS TOO far past midnight and too long before dawn. These are
the terrible hours when ghosts creep out from their hiding places
and show themselves. Some are ghosts who follow Jim from Kellogg,
Idaho. They range free from their dark tombs in the Sunshine silver
mine. They stop their endless flight, their desperate panic to escape.
Jim feels so frustrated with them. Why did they run toward the cen-
tral shaft? That's where the spreading gasses were the worst of the
poison. They should have gone deeper into the mine, back to the
workstations where the emergency breathers and gas masks might
have saved them. Instead, in their panic, they ran right into the waiting arms of Death.

Jim tries not to look at them, tries to shut them out. And somehow, they are gone… But replacing them, appearing from a swirl of
smoke, is a farmer with blind, milky eyes that stare at Jim in confused
sorrow. The man begins to shake, tremors rattling through his body,
wracking him with spasms, until he drops to the dirt floor of his
barn, curls up, and dies. But his eyes, those terrible blind eyes, never
leave Jim.

Now Jim hears the soft ding of an arriving elevator. As he turns
to see the opening doors, he feels himself pushed forward. Jim finds
himself forced into the packed space of the car as a dozen guests are
squeezing in, directed by a hotel bellman. Jim can see by the control

panel they are on the seventh floor. There is a fire on the sixth floor, the bellman warns them. They must go straight to the lobby without stopping. The bellman reaches in and pushes the L button. The doors close, and the elevator starts down.

No one has pushed the button for the sixth floor. There is no reason for the elevator to stop there, no reason why the doors open themselves as the black smoke and searing heat push forward, as the passengers around Jim scream, and the flames rush into the elevator car...

Dripping sweat, Jim lurches up, his breath heaving. He knows the dark room is empty, but he can't be sure until he flips on the bedside light. He gets up, heads to the bathroom, and splashes cold water on his face. He walks back into the room, stands, looking at the bed, at the tangled, sweat-soaked sheets. He feels the weight of exhaustion but can't stand to lie down. He leaves the light on to ensure that there are no lurking shadows, no place for his dead companions to hide.

Jim walks the floor, back and forth, until the sky begins to grow light.

PART THREE

THE GLASS ELEVATOR

22

San Juan Hilton Hotel
January 3, 1987

JIM IS DOWN in the dining room well over an hour before the agreed time he expects Annette, at eight. He doesn't want to order breakfast until she gets there. But after his fourth cup of coffee, he has to order some toast to keep his stomach from eating itself. As he waits, he's been half listening to a morning news show on the TV set above the bar.

A studio announcer is saying, "Federal investigators have determined that arson was the cause of the New Year's Eve fire that killed at least 119 people at the Playa San Juan Hotel, the justice secretary said Sunday…"

A familiar voice gets Jim's attention, and he glances up at the screen. The image has cut to an interviewer, standing before the hotel. He has a microphone in the face of Mike Peralta, identified by a chyron caption as Special Agent in Charge for the FBI in Puerto Rico. Mike is talking.

"We have concluded this was arson, an incendiary fire. The exact cause is under investigation at present. From the evidence so far, we do not conclude that there was any kind of explosive device involved. The sounds reported by witnesses are consistent with the movement of the fire without the involvement of any explosive device…"

"Hey, isn't that Mike?" Jim sees Annette pulling out her chair, her eyes glued to Mike on the screen.

Jim glances at his watch and confirms she is thirty minutes early. He's not surprised.

"However, a special team from the US Treasury Department's Bureau of Alcohol, Tobacco, and Firearms is conducting laboratory tests to confirm the source of ignition…"

"You can tell that guy is single," she says.

"How?"

"FBI or not, no wife would let him out of the house with that tie." As the TV picture switches back to the studio, Annette loses interest. She signals to a waiter for some coffee. "Did they give out a final body count?"

"Still looking. A hundred nineteen and counting, so far."

"I talked to a first-aid guy yesterday. They treated more than a thousand injuries. Some really bad burns. And lots of respiratory cases."

"I expect they could lose quite a few more. Even if they don't find more bodies, the death toll is bound to go up."

Annette sips her coffee. "Maybe we should start our interviews at the hospital? I mean, you know…before we lose any."

Her tone is offhand, and Jim notices she drinks her coffee black. No surprise there. She is clearly not the "sweet and light" type.

"Let's hold off on that for a few days. Don't want to chase any ambulances, so to speak. Doesn't look right."

"Oh…right, of course."

"I want you to get with the tech people from EPA and OSHA today. Make sure they're on the same page for the toxicology reports we need."

"I'm on it. They're still on-site, right?"

"Should be."

"Good. I can pick up a lot just watching them. That's what I like about field work. Books and labs, all that's good, but the real world? That's where you get down to it, you know?"

"You're a real hands-on type, aren't you?"

She takes a menu, and Jim picks up the one that's been in front of him for an hour already.

"Oh, wow," she says. "Look, they have quesitos. Ever try them?"

"Never heard of them."

"I had a lab partner, a great baker, her family came from San Juan. She made quesitos from scratch all the time. It's a little pastry with a dab of cream cheese. Kinda like a Danish, but smaller. You ought to try 'em."

"Sometime. I'll stick to scrambled eggs today."

"Don't want to risk the native food, eh?"

"Lots to do today. Don't want to tempt fate."

"What's on your agenda? I mean, if I may ask. Is that okay?"

"Ask anything and everything. I'm counting on it." She smiles at the confidence he shows in her, and he goes on, "First, I'm looking at some office setups with Valaria. We need enough room for some staff. Couple dozen, maybe more. And interview rooms, where we can record some decent sound."

"Sound, huh? That's important?"

"For depositions? Nothing worse than bad acoustics. You listen to them, one after another, it can drive you crazy."

She smiles and says, "I will remember that."

"You? I get the feeling you'll remember everything."

23

Playa San Juan
January 3, 1987

ANNETTE TOUCHES BASE with the EPA guy first. They talk about residue, how the site cleanup needs to account for the phenyl groups, and the potential harms of benzene. The styrenes are totally nonbiodegradable, and proximity to the beach makes it more essential to avoid contamination. Animals do not recognize polystyrenes as an artificial material. They can mistake it for food. The breakdown products, the smoke and soot from the burning chairs includes isocyanates that can be highly reactive and very caustic, extremely destructive to the organic environment. While polyurethane itself is chemically inert, fire produced significant amounts of hydrogen cyanide, isocyanates, and other toxic residues. These byproducts, the EPA man reminds her, are known carcinogens.

"It'll kill you now or kill you later," he says.

Her conversation with the ATF agents is interesting, but brief. They confirm what she heard from Mike Peralta on TV: no bomb, no explosives.

"You ask me," opines the first agent, "reason we got sent down to check out all this stuff? Teamsters. My, my, how those boys like to blow things up."

The second ATF agent nods vigorously. "Cars especially. You get into a real beef with them? Have somebody else start your car in the morning."

Annette gets into detail with the OSHA techs, who are always interested in a good old deep dive into toxins, so to speak. They compare notes on the condition of the bodies, especially the ones that were not burned to crispy, shrunken husks. They agree on full autopsies on a wide sample, especially the deaths not obviously caused by fire or the blunt force trauma of being trampled. They should have their lungs especially tested and investigated and samples preserved. She knows from Jim that the objective of their defense strategy is to establish solid evidence that the liability for the hotel should be reduced, or at least shared, especially for some of the deaths that are the result of toxic chemicals. That may provide a chance to pin at least some of the cost to the makers of the furniture pads that produced those toxic gases.

She breaks off this geek-out session when she spots Mike Peralta. He's over on the perimeter, by the forensic tents, and she does her best to look casual as she heads in his direction. It wouldn't hurt to apply some solid scientific field work to confirm or deny her hypothesis about those horrible ties.

"Hi there, Special Agent," she says, walking up to him. She offers her hand. "Annette Rowan. We met yesterday?"

"Sure, of course. And Mike is just fine."

"Okay. Mike then."

"You're with Jim Feller."

"Guilty."

"You do know the guy is a legend, right?"

"Have you worked on cases with him before?"

"Not me. But Billy Chertoff has. Good friend of mine, used to be the SAC in our Las Vegas office. He has all kinds of stories about your Jimbo."

"Like what?"

"Oh, man. That MGM fire? Billy had to detail two, three guys to keep eyes on Jim out there. I mean, around the clock."

"Why? What did he do?"

"He pissed off some bad people. Way Billy puts it? Sometimes Jim kind of forgets he's a lawyer, not a law man."

Annette can tell Peralta thinks that's a really bad idea, on one hand, but she also detects that he can't help admiring Jim for this.

"You're saying he takes too many chances?"

"Well…he's not careless or anything like that. He just tends to push the wrong people's buttons sometimes. There's a time to poke the bear and a time to stay the hell out of the cave."

"I take it that's your job, then? Are you good at poking?"

"I get paid to take those chances. He doesn't need to." He looks at her, and again she notices how those eyes of his can drill down into you. "You don't either. Okay?"

"I'm pretty sure you can handle trouble just fine." She can tell he likes hearing her say that. She also notices she's right about the shirt. Only no-iron polyester could look that crisp in this heat. Then she realizes how she is kind of staring at him and changes the subject to avoid blushing. "So, Mike, settle a bet for me."

"A bet? What do you…"

"Never mind, that's just an expression. I was wondering…the ties. When you get ready to leave the house in the morning, do you pick out your own tie?"

"Sure," he says, puzzled. "Why wouldn't I?"

She shrugs. "No reason at all," and that is just fine with her.

Standing outside the police tape surrounding the hotel property, Luis Ortiz stares at the charred ruins of his life. His twenty years of hard work in the kitchen of the Playa San Juan are gone. His future, his dream of running the kitchen himself one day? Gone. And Sofia… In his heart, he wants to believe she isn't gone, she can't be. Only as the days go by, he is losing his grip on that hope. True, there is a list of the dead, and she is still not on that list. But he knows there are still almost fifty bodies that have not been identified yet.

Today is the third day in a row Luis checks her apartment, their little hideaway, the place they take that short five-minute walk to every chance they get. Again, no one is there, like yesterday and the day before. But today he sees Anita. Fat, happy Anita, Sofia's next-door neighbor. She is watering the sorry-looking flowers in her window box. He thinks about asking her if she has seen Sofia but loses his courage and turns to leave.

But Anita calls to him, "Luis! Are you here to meet her? Is she coming home?"

"I...I don't..." His words choke off. If he admits he doesn't think so, if he gives voice to this terrible, inevitable thought, then it will be true. So he can't say it, won't say it. "I don't know. Keep your fingers crossed."

He turns and walks away quickly, trying to keep ahead of the tears.

San Juan
January 3, 1987

"I think this next place we're going to see is the best one available," Valaria says. Jim is grateful that she's being so helpful. But she is starting to sound like a real estate agent. "It's less than half a mile from the Playa, and it's only a ten-minute walk for you from the Hilton."

"Is it bigger than that the last place you showed us? We're going to need more room than that one had."

"Oh, this one is much bigger and a nicer building. It's located on the top floor, with great views. Only two years old, has great plumbing, wiring, and that's stuff you can't always take for granted down here."

"I could tell from the other places," he says, remembering the faint but unpleasant smells at the last place they looked at.

Jim remembers real estate techniques way back from one of his law classes. Show your second-best property first, the worst one second. Then on the last stop, you show them the best one. Jim knows Valaria's background. She never sold real estate, that's for sure. But she clearly picked up the tricks of the trade somewhere. Then again, he figures, there probably isn't too much she's not good at.

They sit in the comfortable, spacious back of her Lincoln, relaxing on the soft black leather seats, cool as you please in the air-conditioning. Up in front, her driver has the news playing low on the radio. Jim catches something, and asks the driver to turn it up a bit.

"Questions at the news conference. The Teamster spokesman also repeated the union's denial of any role in the fatal hotel fire. In addition, Feliciano said the Teamsters have offered a fifteen-thousand-dollar reward for information leading to the arrest of the arsonists and pledges the union will continue to cooperate with investigators. He dismissed any suggestions that might connect the arson with recent labor unrest between the union's hotel workers and—"

The driver switches off the radio as the Lincoln turns onto Calle Mille Flores and pulls into the parking lot of a sleek, modern office building. The exterior has that popular dark metal and glass look, with lots of windows. There is a wide, shaded entrance, and the first thing he notices is a very distinctive feature on the exterior: two large, tower-like columns set off on either side of the front doors.

The glass elevators shafts.

The glassed-in passenger cars can be seen going up and down inside the transparent elevator shafts, which are all windows on three sides. The passengers inside, rather than feeling confined in small, claustrophobic boxes, have a full view of the outside as they are carried to their floors. It gives the whole structure a futuristic look, almost too cosmopolitan for the historic charm of the old Spanish city of San Juan. But it sure looks cool, Jim admits to himself. As they go inside, he notices the name on the building: Crystal Towers Office Plaza.

The place turns out to be perfect. There is virtually no build-out necessary, as the prior tenant was a law firm.

"The only reason they left," Valaria confides, "is that they did so well they outgrew the place. They would have expanded right here if they could, but all the other floors are full, and the tenants are all too happy to move out."

As they walk through the space, Jim is very favorably impressed. There are two very spacious corner offices, "partner offices," Valaria calls them, and A dozen other private offices for some of the expert staff, the team of specialists Jim plans to bring in. This elite group is one Jim assembled over the years, a team of fire investigators which includes the best forensic scientists, engineers, and researchers in the country. These are his "team"—people Jim assembled and worked with successfully on dozens of cases over more than two decades. He also relies on a team of seasoned young lawyers who master the art of tracking down and interviewing witnesses, friendly and otherwise. They work in concert with a staff of researchers who have the legal skills to clerk for any judge in any court in the country. And they are especially talented when it comes to sleuthing out the hundreds and hundreds of witnesses they will need to interview.

Obviously, with their hotel burned out, many of the surviving hotel staff of the Playa San Juan will scatter across the whole island, not to mention crossing to the mainland in search of new jobs. Not only will they have to track down former hotel staff but they'll have to locate and contact hundreds of guests. These included the whole spectrum of snowbird tourists who flock to the Playa (or used to) from all over. Many come down to escape frigid New England, the chilly Midwest, the wintery East Coast, and from all over the United States, not to mention Europe. Valaria compiles a complete list of the international guests who were checked in at the time of the blaze. They come from as far as Spain, Great Britain, Brussels, Stockholm, Argentina, even Australia. Some will come to them, already lawyered up and looking for damages. Others will need to be hunted down. Statements, interrogatories, interviews, depositions—the task will be gargantuan. Jim's handpicked support staff has a variety of specialized skills, including medical experts, forensic accountants, even psychological evaluators—an entire army.

But this office suite will be sufficient to pull them all together in one effective work environment. Besides the good-sized office pool and over a dozen small private and semi-private offices, there are two large conference rooms and one room dedicated to recording interviews. It seems to be modeled on a police interrogation room, including a one-way mirror, allowing unseen observers to monitor the interviews. But the big selling point is that this room is set up perfectly for sound recording, with acoustical ceilings, carpeted floors, and even sound baffles on the walls.

As they complete their walk-through, Valaria enjoys the chance to ask, "So? What do you think? Can you make it work?"

"I suppose it will have to do," he deadpans. Jim smiles at the self-satisfied expression on Valaria's face. It's a look she has earned. Then he smiles back, adding, "Heck, we could form a garage band and cut a demo in here."

He holds up his palm, and she takes him up on the invitation, slapping him a high five.

As they ride back down from their inspection in the glass elevator, Jim takes in the view of the surrounding neighborhood. The street has a few other office complexes, several commercial warehouses, and a few modest coffee shops and small restaurants.

"Any of these decent places to eat?"

"I suppose so. And you did notice our break-room area?"

"Not too shabby," he says. "Almost too nice. I'll probably need an armed guard to shoo people back to their work."

"It's practically a full kitchen already. A few improvements, and you could bring in a chef to feed the whole office right there."

"Things might get so busy I'll need to bring in cots and make them sleep at the office." She reaches into her attaché and hands him a sheet of paper. He looks; it's some kind of list. "What's this?"

"Those are the four best security firms in San Juan. I can vouch for any of them, including this one," she says, pointing at a name. "I know they're good. I hired them for the Playa, and they did a good job."

"Except for the little matter of a fire."

"I don't know what they could have done to stop that. After all, the Teamsters who set that fire? They worked for the hotel. It's not like security failed to identify some nefarious characters sneaking around. And the security chief, Delgado? His people saved a lot of lives. He lost three of them fighting the fire. They're good men. And I know they could use the work."

"Okay. I'll meet with him."

"Thank you," she says. "Now. Should we try out one of these local greasy spoons to see it they can manage not to poison us?"

"Are you buying?"

24

Crystal Towers Office Plaza
January 7, 1987

ANNETTE WEAVES HER way through the bustling bedlam of move-in day, dodging through a beehive, between furniture dollies loaded with desks, copiers, credenzas; weaving past the divider walls going up, filling in the office pool like a growing labyrinth. She passes Jim's corner office, sees that he's busy in a meeting with Rubén Delgado, their newly hired chief security officer. She gives a fast wave and runs the obstacle course to her own corner office. She looks around at it. Empty still. It looks huge. This whole operation is huge and growing crazier by the day.

She stands at one of the huge windows in her spacious office. She gazes absently out onto Calle Mille Flores. A quiet street, not much traffic. Her mind drifts as she remembers back, just two days ago. The whole place is still deserted then. The only furniture is in Jim's office, where he's already at work, sitting at a big plastic folding table, with card chairs scattered around. He is interviewing security firms. Annette feels proud when he asks her to sit in on the sessions with each of the three companies. When they finish the last interview, Jim turns to her and asks her opinion. This flatters her, but more importantly, it reinforces her sense that he values her judgment. And she has an answer ready.

"I say Delgado," she tells him.

"The guys from Playa?" He nods thoughtfully. "Okay. Why? Talk me through your reasons."

She likes the way he does this. When he asks her opinion, he always makes her reason through why she thinks that way, interested in the evidence to support her ideas. Always wanting to hear her supporting argument.

"Delgado seems motivated," she says. "Like he feels that fire happened on his watch, and he wants to make it up. A personal obligation, I guess."

"I tend to agree with you. It's obvious he doesn't have much love for the Teamsters either. If we do have any problems, it will come from them."

"Plus, Mike likes the guy," she adds.

Jim looks at her a second then asks, "Mike?"

"Peralta. I asked him."

"The FBI man? When did you talk to him?"

"Oh, I ran into him, down at the site. We chatted. You know."

"You just chatted with the FBI? About what?"

"A few things. Hotel security. Teamsters. You."

"Me?"

"Yeah. And neckties. I was right, he buys his own."

"Wait, back up," Jim says, trying to follow her.

"We had a drink later."

"You did what?"

"He's very nice. And he likes you."

"Me? I don't even know the guy."

"Well, he knows all about you. Thinks you're a cowboy."

"I'm a... What are you talking about?"

"He didn't say that exactly. But he knows you have a hard on about the Teamsters. From Las Vegas, he said."

Now it makes sense to Jim. "Hell. He's been talking to Billy Chertoff."

"That's right. How'd you know?"

"I know Billy. He's a gossipy old lady." Jim shakes his head. "Look, I don't know what Mike told you. It's no secret I don't much care for Teamsters. As for Las Vegas... Yeah, I had some trouble with them. But it's not a personal thing. It's got nothing to do with this job. We have a case to focus on here."

"And they started the fire."

"Listen. There's nothing I'd like better than to pin this fire on them. Because it's in our client's best interest."

"Mm-hmm," she says, managing to convey her opinion without actually rolling her eyes at that one.

"The point is, I plan to be careful. And I want you to be careful too. These guys are thugs. You stay clear of them, understand?"

"Me? You think I'm crazy?"

"No, no, I don't mean… Look, I know you wouldn't do anything stupid, confront them, anything like that. But just…keep your eyes open, that's all."

"You trying to scare me now?"

"Damn right."

"Don't worry, Boss. I'm a chicken heart to the core." She smiles. Then as she starts to leave, she adds, "Besides, I have a guardian angel."

Jim calls after her, "What's that supposed to mean?"

Her only answer is to wink at him and keep going.

Still in her office, Annette startles from her reverie.

A big lug of a mover hovers in the doorway, with a magnificent teak desk strapped to a dolly, and asks, "Where do you want this?"

She makes up her mind. "Not in here. Hang on."

Delgado is just leaving Jim's office as she walks in. She carries an office floor plan with her, and she spreads it out on Jim's desk.

"I don't want that big ass office way down there, halfway to Timbuktu," she says, pointing at it.

"What's wrong with it? I thought—"

She interrupts him, pointing at the plan, "See? Right here? This is where the real fire investigators are: the chemist, the engineer, all the forensic guys. I want to be there with them."

"Well, but… Those offices, they're kind of crowded."

"I don't care about that. I want to be where they are. I don't want to miss anything they're doing." She looks at Jim now and smiles. "I know you want me to feel I'm…that I mean something. Really, I appreciate it. But a big office? Doesn't do a thing for me. If you want me to give you my best? Put me where I can do the most good."

Jim shakes his head. "Young woman, you don't know the first damn thing about office politics, do you?"

"And I never want to."

"Well…let's fix up this floor plan and get you moved in."

25

Crystal Towers Office Plaza
January 10, 1987

IT'S NOT A very hot day, partly cloudy, a nice breeze. But even though the sun isn't beating down as usual, Manny Huerta feels the sweat trickle down his back and is very aware of the large wet spots on his shirt under each arm. He had tried to make sure this appointment was set up for his day off, and they had done that. Then yesterday his new boss tells him the schedule is changing, and he needs to work today. He tries to get these investigation people to change his appointment again, but they say they can't. So he has to take personal time off. He has to tell his boss, who doesn't like it, gets all up in his face.

He doesn't want to piss off his new boss. This new job of his at the Marriott is a lot better than washing dishes at the Playa too. Plus, the Marriott is easier for him to get to from his place. The pay's better too. The union really came through for him, got him juiced in for this new spot at another hotel just three days after the Playa burned. He feels grateful. They're taking good care of him. His new boss runs an easy kitchen compared to how hard old Luis worked him at the Playa.

Not that Luis isn't a good boss too. He is. A smart guy too. Manny remembers how Luis is always tough on him, but the way he does it always makes it clear he cares about Manny, that he wants him to do better for himself. He wonders what's happening with

Luis. Where is he now? Did he get a new job in a different hotel? He feels a little bit bad for the guy, knows Luis had worked his way up at the Playa, how the old guy believes he'll be running the whole kitchen one day. Now it's gone for good. He hopes Luis doesn't lose all the rank he worked so hard to build up for all those years. But maybe the union will take good care of Luis too. The guy needs a break too. Manny hears Luis is really busted up about that waitress he was screwing, Sofia. Poor girl got fried so bad it took four days to identify the body.

This whole thing with the fire? It's all fucked up, man. Manny knows what people are saying, but he doesn't believe it. Besides, if the union had anything to do with it… He's not saying they did, of course, not even thinking it. But whatever happened, he doesn't know anything about it, doesn't know why these people investigating everything even want to talk to him. He doesn't know crap.

And that's exactly what he tells the union rep. The guy takes such good care of him, gets him this new spot at Marriott. Manny just tells the guy the truth. He's at the union meeting, goes there just like his shop steward tells him to do. He's down there in the lower ballroom, has no idea what starts that fight right before the fire. He's just standing there, listening to the brass talk a lot of shit about the contract, like everybody else is. Then all of a sudden, people are hitting each other. And then…then that screaming… *Fire…*

It's terrible. He still hears all that screaming, can't help it. And the stink? Like someone forgets to pull a roast out of the oven. And all that black shit, that smoke which almost chokes him. He still has a cough, and it hurts to breathe sometimes. It's so goddamn scary, he remembers, like he's going to die if he doesn't get the hell away from there. But he can't run, can hardly walk, not with that smoke. He's never been so scared.

But right now? It's a different kind of fear. He feels this watery gut pain and a chill behind his neck, like a shiver. His hands are shaky too. It's bad, almost as bad as during the fire.

The difference? Manny doesn't really know why he's so scared now. What are they going to ask him? He doesn't know nothing. And that's all he should say. That's what his boss told him to say. You don't know shit, and that's all you give 'em.

He goes into the building, Crystal Towers. As he starts to ride up in that weird elevator, with all the glass, that scary feeling gets even worse.

It almost feels like somebody is watching him.

26

Interview Room
Crystal Towers Office Plaza

Transcription of Interview

Interview Date: January 10, 1987
Location: Law Office of Marcos & Feller, LLP
272 Calle Romero=Suite 500
San Juan, Puerto Rico
Interview of Manuel Huerta (MH)
Interviewed by James Feller (JF)
Annette Rowan (AR)
Valaria Marcos (VM)
SAC Michael Peralta (MP)

On January 9. 1987, James Feller, Annette Rowan, and Valaria
Marcos interviewed Manuel Huerta at the Law Office of Marcos &
Feller, LLP. Also present was FBI SAC Michael Peralta with consent
of all parties.

VM: It is presently 1134 hours on January 10, 1987. Present are myself, Valaria Marcos, along with James Feller and Annette Rowan, currently with ad hoc law firm of Marcos & Feller LLP to interview Manuel Huerta. Also present is FBI SAC Michael Peralta with the consent of all parties. This interview is being recorded with the consent of all parties. Mr. Huerta, thank you for coming in today.

MH: Oh, yes, you're welcome.

VM: I'd like to start out by getting some basic information down. Your name is spelled M-A-N-U-E-L and Huerta, H-U-E-R-T-A, correct?

MH: Yes, ma'am, that's right.

VM: And on the day of the fire, you were employed in the kitchen of the Playa San Juan Hotel?

MH: Yeah... I mean, yes, I was on duty from 8:00 a.m. to 4:00 p.m. Well, I guess the fire started, I mean, I don't know if you'd say I was, like, working? Once the fire started, you know?

VM: That's fine, Mr. Huerta, we just—

MH: It's Manny. I mean, you can call me that, everyone calls me Manny.

VM: All right then. Manny. And you are a member of Local 901 of the International Brotherhood of Teamsters, Manny, is that correct?

MH: Yeah. They already got me a new job, you know, since... I work at Marriott now.

VM: Thank you. And is your present address still 2218 Aveneda Barcelona, apartment 339?

MH: That's right. And it's closer to Marriott. I mean, compared to the Playa. So that's better, you know?

VM: Yes, I understand. Now, Manny, this is Jim Feller, and the lady is Annette Rowan. The gentlemen over there is Special Agent in Charge of the San Juan field office of the FBI, Michael Peralta. You are aware this interview is being recorded, and you have given permission. Correct?

MH: Yes, ma'am. That's okay.

VM: All right then. Mr. Feller is going to ask you some questions about the day of the fire. If you don't know the answer, or don't remember, that's fine, just say so. Or if you are not sure, you can say that. Don't guess or anything, just answer to the best of your ability. And if you don't understand the question, just say so. Do you understand?

MH: I get it, yeah. I'll do my best.

JF: Thank you, Manny. I'm Jim Feller. My associate, Annette Rowan, and I are attorneys for the owners of the Playa San Juan hotel. Now, on December 31, 1986, can you tell us what you were doing at around three in the afternoon, please.

MH: Okay, sure. Well, I was at the meeting...

JF: That would be the meeting of your Local 901?

MH: Right. See, I was in the kitchen, and around an hour before, Rosa comes by.

JF: And who is she?

MH: No, hah. Don't say that to him! Efrain Rosa, he's a union rep. He comes by and tells me to come to the lower ballroom at 2:30. They were having a meeting about the new contract, he says, and he wants all of us to show up. It was okay with the hotel, he said. We didn't even have to punch out. It was still on the clock. Luis was there with me, in the kitchen. Luis Ortiz, he's old, like forty-something. He's been at the Playa forever. So anyway, he tells me to blow off the meeting, it's all bullshit. Tells me all about how they're going to fuck over the Playa and go on strike, no matter what. He don't care what the Teamsters say, he ain't going 'cause it's New Year's Eve, and he's all busy and shit. Tells me go ahead, take the break, get paid for it. Then just go have a beer and a smoke.

JF: But you went to the union meeting anyway?

MH: Well, yeah... I mean, I don't wanna get Rosa all pissed. He's a real...

JF: Go ahead. About Rosa.

MH: Nothing, only like I said, you don't want him pissed at you, that guy. He's all juiced in, ya know?

JF: You mean, he's in tight with Teamsters leadership?

MH: That's right.

JF: So you wanted to be sure he saw that you attended the meeting?

MH: Right.

AR: And did you?

MH: Ma'am? Sorry?

AR: At the meeting. Did you see Mr. Rosa at the meeting?

MH: Uh...did I... I don't think so. I don't remember seeing him anyway...

27

Interview Room
Crystal Towers Office Plaza

IT'S AROUND FOUR thirty in the afternoon, and the last interview subject of the day is just leaving. As the door closes behind him, Jim, Annette, and the others are gathering up their notes, stretching, sipping at water bottles.

"Good day," Jim says. "For a first day anyway."

Valaria asks, "Do you want me to get these tapes transcribed or…"

"No, no, thanks," Jim says. "I have plenty of people in house here. That's what they're for." *And I know my people won't leave anything out,* he thinks. "I do have a question about the list for tomorrow," says Jim.

Annette has a copy in front of her already. Of course.

"What is it, Boss?"

"Please don't call me that anymore."

"Okay. Guv'ner."

Jim rolls his eyes. "I thought we were going to talk to the hotel's general manager tomorrow. I don't see his name on here."

"He cancelled. Says he needs to reschedule," Annette tells him.

Jim turns to Valaria. "You know anything about this?"

"Me? Why should I?"

"These hotel people. They're your people. Tell this guy I need to talk to him. Tomorrow. It's not optional."

"Sure. Of course." She busies herself with her briefcase and then says, offhand, "You're talking about Rodriguez, right?"

"Humberto Rodriguez, that's right."

"I'll let him know. But…just out of curiosity, why is he so urgent? From what I understand, he wasn't even on duty for the whole week before the fire. He was off from Christmas through"— she pauses, realizing—"well, obviously, he's still off. There's no hotel to manage."

"I understand. I just need him to clear up some general things. Who's responsible for what, things like that. I don't mean the organizational chart but who really runs things. You know what I mean?"

"I'll get on him."

"Thanks."

As she leaves, Jim hears a snicker of laughter behind him. He turns, but he can see it has nothing to do with him. Annette and Mike Peralta are doing a mocking imitation of the bell captain they interviewed earlier, a nasal-sounding guy who was quite the pompous ass.

As Mike notices Jim looking at them, he goes all serious "Thanks for letting me sit in, Jim. I still plan to call in a couple of these people myself, but I can definitely weed out a few of them after today."

"I'm interested in this union guy."

"Rosa." Mike nods. "So am I."

"Interesting that Manny Huerta didn't see him at the meeting. I wonder where he was?"

"He's supposed to come in on…" Annette consults her paperwork. "Day after tomorrow. Think he'll show up?"

Mike smiles. "I almost hope he doesn't. That might say something." Mike picks up his suit jacket, which hangs on the back of his chair. As he shrugs into it, he says, "Okay, see you later."

Jim is about to answer, but then he realizes Mike is talking directly to Annette.

She smiles back at him and says, "I'll be in the lobby at seven thirty."

"No, no. I'm doing okay," Julie tells Jim over the phone.

Jim calls her every night from his room in the Hilton. Right now, he's in his swim trunks, wearing a robe with the Hilton logo, with a towel over his shoulder.

"Have you heard anything from Ellen yet?"

"Oh, yes, yes. I forgot to tell you. She called last night. They got in just fine. Apparently, her friend Sondra is a terrible driver. And has a weak bladder. Ellen says they must have stopped twenty times between here and Oberlin. But at least they made it there safe and sound."

"And how's Sarah?"

"Her flight to New Orleans was okay. She ran into a friend at the airport, and they shared a cab to campus. Haven't heard anything else since she got in. Tulane has their finals week coming up, and she's apparently on the bubble in her English class. Or is it history? Something she wants an A in anyway."

"Well, that could be anything. Good thing she has your brains."

"Not only that, she was lucky enough not to get your looks."

"Small blessings. I tried calling her yesterday, but I just got her damn answering machine again."

"Well, you're the one who gave it to her for Christmas."

"Maybe she'll return a call for my birthday."

"Aww. Poor baby."

"At least she calls you." Then, not kidding now, he adds, "And I'm really glad she does, Jewel. Never mind grumpy, old me. Your girls love you very much. Always will."

"I know... I just miss them. And you too...but only a little bit."

"I'll take it."

"Are you eating right? You better be. If you get fat, don't bother coming home."

"Me? I'm on my way to the pool to swim laps right now."

"Don't drown." But then her voice is more serious. "Jim? Do be careful, okay? Take care of yourself. I love you."

"I love you more, Jewel. Bye."

Jim likes coming down to the pool late for his swim. It's a good end to his day and helps him push through the stress of the day's work. The pool stays open until ten. Back when they checked in, the manager told him not to worry about that. He can start his swim after the pool's closed; he's welcome to complete his workout, which takes only about thirty minutes anyway.

Tonight it's nearly midnight when he gets down to the pool area. The advantage of starting so late is there's never anybody down at the pool when he gets here. So there's never a worry about plowing into some orthodontist from Toledo while he churns through his paces. The hotel keeps the water warmer than he prefers because the workout heats him up, so he'd like it a bit cooler.

As usual, tonight the whole pool area is deserted. Once the pool closes, the lighting is turned down quite low. Mostly the only light comes from landscape spots to paint the palms with a glow or highlight fronds and flowers. But the underwater lights in the pool are on, and their sparkle makes the water look even more inviting. Jim tosses his large, plush towel on a chaise, along with the fluffy terrycloth robe from the hotel. He hops into the warm pool.

By habit, he always does a crawl stroke for one length, does a fairly respectable kick turn, and the breaststrokes back. Alternating strokes gives his workout just a bit of variation and keeps it from getting boring. He's been at it around fifteen minutes now, into a good rhythm. By this time, the routine of the laps clears his mind. The term *meditation* always strikes Jim as a little bit too hippie for him. But the effect of the repetition in his workout, the pure focus on movement, on his regular pattern of breathing, always has that same effect, whatever you want to call it: a deep, clear calm; a peaceful pause from the bombardment of thoughts; a break for his active mind.

While doing his crawl stroke, his head is mostly down in the water, with only the quick turn of his head every other stroke for a breath. So later, when he thinks about it, he understands why he never saw it happening.

He reaches the end of his crawl lap, does his flip turn, and starts back in the other direction. As he breaststrokes back to the opposite end of the pool, his head pops up out of the water for each breath, facing forward. As he sucks air in deeply, it's the smell he notices first.

That's what alerts him, makes him pull up and actually look around over at the pool deck.

They must have used gasoline or maybe charcoal starter, something that gets his robe and towel burning hot and fast, like a torch. Instantly Jim hops from the pool, scanning the deck area for something he can use to douse the flames, maybe an ice bucket or even a child's toy pail, but there's nothing. He spies a bin full of used towels. He grabs a couple, dunks them in the pool, pulls them out soaking wet. He flops one saturated towel over the flaming chair, and then another, drowning the flames. A cloud of hissing steam mixes with the scorched stink of the chair's burned plastic slats.

As soon as the fire is out, Jim's head is on a swivel. But it's no surprise that he finds the entire pool-deck area still deserted. Or, to be more correct, it's deserted again.

The actual physical damage is quite minimal, as it was no doubt intended. But it's not just the night air on his wet skin that gives Jim a shiver.

The message has been delivered. It's game on.

28

Interview Room
Crystal Towers Office Plaza

As THEY GET ready to resume their interviews, Jim takes Annette
aside. He talks quietly, his voice low. He tells her about the fire by
the pool.

She looks more angry than frightened. "Screw them…right?"

"We're not going to back off our investigation, but I want you
to be double careful. On your guard, okay?"

"When I went to MIT? I couldn't afford to live in nice, safe
Cambridge. I had to share a place in Roxbury. Ever been to Roxbury?"

"I haven't spent much time in Boston."

"Only neighborhood worse is Dorchester. I know, I had a waitress job in Dorchester." Shows him an aerosol mini can of Mace she
pulls from her bag. "This came in handy more than once."

Jim thinks she is deflecting and wants her to take this more
seriously.

"I'm glad you know how to take care of yourself. Just don't let a
nice office building or a comfortable hotel fool you. It's all Roxderry
around here."

"Roxbury."

"Point is, the Teamsters don't give a damn. They can turn up
anywhere."

Seeing the worry in his face, she is touched. "Okay. And thank
you. I appreciate that you care."

"I'm sorry if I sounded harsh. I tried to let you know last night. And I was… I got worried when you didn't answer the door. It was after midnight."

"Gee, Dad. I didn't know I had a curfew." She sees him start to react again and laughs. "Kidding. I'm kidding. I'll be careful, I promise."

The interviews continue. In the afternoon, they depose Humberto Rodriguez, the Playa's general manager. As usual, Valaria does the opening boilerplate, name, address, permission to record, all that. But as she does, Rodriguez strikes Jim as defensive, almost insulted, that he is here being questioned.

"I wasn't even in the city, you know. My wife's family, they own property outside Dorado. I didn't even hear about the fire until the day after New Year's."

"I'm aware of that," Jim says. "I still have some other questions you can help me with. Procedural things."

"Such as?"

"Do you know why the furniture, the new stuff that burned, was being stored in the upper ballroom."

"For safekeeping."

Jim waits. Rodriguez doesn't add anything.

"Safekeeping. From…"

"I think you know the answer."

"I think I'd like to know your answer."

Rodriguez turns to Valaria, almost on appeal. "Why is this man trying to put the blame on me? This is most irregular. You are supposed to be on our side here."

"Humberto, please. This is a serious investigation. We are just trying to find out all the facts. It's not personal."

"I feel I am being accused."

Jim tries to steer the interview back on track by asking, "Mr. Rodriguez, is it true that you had the new furniture moved inside the upper ballroom because you feared it could be vandalized by the Teamsters union?"

"Yes, well, obviously."

"And could you explain why? Just for our records?"

"As you know, the owners had plans for extensive renovations after the high season ended. We took delivery on the new furniture months in advance of when it was needed because the manufacturer needed to clear their inventory. They gave us a very good price to take it immediately. At first, we had it in some roll-off shipping container units, what do they call them…SeaLand trailers, sitting in the parking area. That was an eyesore, for one thing. But the main concern was, as you say, the Teamsters. It's no secret that they are known to commit various… They try to intimidate ownership during negotiations. The upper ballroom became available due to seasonal factors. It doesn't get any use during the holiday season. So it just seemed the best way to get that stuff out of sight and under lock and key. Is there something wrong with that?"

"Not in the least. And to answer your other concern, we are not trying to find ways to blame anything on you or the hotel. My objective is to establish a reasonable suspicion that the Teamsters are responsible for the fire."

"Oh. Yes, I see. I'm sorry. Please, ask anything, I will help you if I can."

Jim walks him through a number of other issues: Does the staff ever conduct fire drills? Are there any directions or maps posted to direct people to the nearest exits? Are there protocols for procedures during emergencies? As the pattern emerges, it becomes clear that fire safety planning had not been a priority at Playa San Juan.

"Were there fire or smoke alarms in the upper ballroom?"

"No."

"How about fire sprinkler systems?"

"No, those are not required—"

"In the casino?"

"No, but—"

"What about the guest rooms or the hallways?"

"We have smoke alarms in the kitchen."

"How about the lobby? The restaurants?"

"We comply with all the necessary building codes. The alarms you are asking about are not required under code here."

"You said extensive upgrades to the property are planned. Do these upgrades include plans for smoke alarms or fire sprinklers?"

Rodriguez shoots another dirty look at Valaria who shrugs. "You might as well answer him, 'Berto."

"The renovation plans did not include adding those things, no."

Jim lets that sit. He turns and nods to Annette. From her well-organized folder of documents, she produces a document, shows it to Jim, then slides it across to Valaria to show it to Rodriguez.

"For my next questions, I refer you to this diagram here. It shows the floor plan of the casino. Are you familiar with the layout of the casino area?"

"Yes, of course."

"You can see on the plans where it indicates the areas of slot machines, the roulette wheels, craps tables, blackjack, poker, the cashier cage, the bars, restrooms, entrance and exit doors. Does this diagram appear roughly accurate to you?"

"It looks about right."

"And if you'll look at the west wall, that's the side on the left, there are two sets of exit doors. Near the bar, there. See them?"

"I see them."

"When we inspected the site of the fire, we found that these exit doors had been locked. In fact, they were chained shut and padlocked. Were you aware of this?"

"That's only… That is a security issue. Was."

"Yes, we asked Captain Delgado, your former chief of security, about this. He said they were locked shut like that before his tenure began. For years, in fact. Did Captain Delgado bring to your attention that blocking these exits might constitute a hazard in an emergency?"

"I told him, look, the reason for locking them, they are right next to the bar, you can see that."

"Captain Delgado said you told him the doors were to remain locked in spite of his objections. Is that correct?"

"I had good reason to—" He stops himself. "We had tremendous problems with theft. Liquor was going out the back door as fast as we could stock it. The pilferage was unacceptable. It was thousands of dollars every month."

"I see. And so is it correct to say you decided the exit doors there would remain locked—chained shut—to save money? Correct?"

When the interview is finally over, Rodriguez mutters furious curses at Valaria. But his fury doesn't mask the shame that has him on the verge of tears. He slams the door on his way out of the interview room.

By the time he reaches the glass elevator and it starts down, he is wiping tears from his eyes.

That night Kiko arrives at the Teamster headquarters, carrying a VHS tape. He crosses through the open plan office pool to the door in the rear. He moves through the gloom of the semi-darkened utility room toward the light which spills from the open door of the office in the back.

Beltran is on the phone, but when he sees Kiko with the VHS tape, he excuses himself and hangs up.

"That's today's?"

"Right."

"Let's have a look."

Kiko turns on a TV on a rolling stand and puts the tape into the VCR hooked up to the set. He pushes the play button.

It's been a very long day, Annette thinks as she and Jim return to the Hilton. He asks her if she wants to join him for a drink.

"Thanks, but not tonight," she says, offhand, as she walks quickly to the elevator.

As she presses the button for her floor, she can't seem to shake the feeling she's had ever since Jim dragged the story of the locked doors out of Rodriguez, the hotel manager. When the elevator doors open, she steps out and starts down the hall toward her room. She can't stop herself from glancing up at the hallway ceiling. No sprinklers. No smoke alarms. It gives her a chill. As a reflex, she wonders what other hazards this hotel has ignored.

She pulls out her room key and hesitates before opening the door. Should she check out the exit doors? The stairwell? How easy is it to get out of this building?

For that matter, how easy is it to get in?

She shakes off the uncomfortable, worrying thought. Silly.

Opening the door, she steps into the darkened room, her hand feeling along the wall for the light switch. A hand grabs her wrist and pulls her suddenly, and she crashes into a big, hard body. Powerful arms instantly encircle her as she is lifted off her feet and onto the bed.

"You're late," the man says, his lips brushing her ear as his hands begin to roam over her body.

"Oh Mike, you nearly scared me to death. I must admit it's a turn on, though."

29

Bario Playita
San Juan

Manny Huerta has a hard time finding the street where the modest, three-bedroom bungalow of Luis Ortiz is tucked away. Three different people have given him instructions how to find the cul-de-sac, but an absence of signs and lack of street lights has Manny wandering for an hour.

But finally, he recognizes the battered old Datsun, showing more primer than finished paint, that he's seen Luis drive to work so many times.

Fat and somber, Luis's wife, Effie, opens the door with a nervous caution. Her surprise gives way to a look of resigned despair, which she tries to hide with a forced smile.

"Manny? Is that you?"

"Ola, Mrs. Ortiz. It's nice to see you again." In fact, he thinks to himself, it's painful to see her. The woman looks like a lumpy, over-stuffed sack of misery on bad legs.

"Please, please, come in," she mumbles, ushering Manny inside. She leads him through the dim, cluttered interior. She mutters in a voice that personifies chronic suffering, with the occasional bright spot of mere sadness, "What a blessing to have you drop by. I don't know what to do with him. He is a broken man. He barely gets out of bed. Won't eat. Imagine it. Luis? The man lived for food. I don't have to tell you."

What a perfect match for you then, Manny thinks then regrets the unkind thought.

"I practically had to drag him out to the patio," she says as she slides open the door to a small enclosed backyard. It brims with colorful flowers and appears to be home to a spectacular blue-and-gold macaw. The space would be a cheerful oasis, if Luis wasn't blackening the atmosphere with the shade of his obvious depression. Effie uses a low voice to say, "I know it will cheer him up to see you," not low enough that Luis doesn't plainly hear her and shrink a little deeper into himself.

There is another chair near the seat Luis has melted his body into. Manny is about to sit, but he decides to drag the chair over close to his old boss. He tries to find a trace of Luis in the man, the Luis he knows, the man who can always find the spark in everyone, find that one bright spot of promise. Manny only now realizes how much he misses having Luis Hector prod him to do better, to reach higher, to take pride in even the lowest task. It takes him until the constant prodding is gone to realize Luis wasn't finding fault with Manny; he was trying to push the young man to find himself, find that there was more inside him.

But now what Manny sees slumping in that chair is exactly what his wife describes, a broken man.

Manny puts a hand gently on the knee of his old mentor. His quiet acceptance of the man's profound sadness speaks with a kind of eloquence words can't match. Finally, Luis raises his filmy eyes to Manny. He gives the smallest nod, acknowledging his appreciation for the young man's understanding.

"Thank you for coming, son."

"I miss your scolding, old devil. There's no one to kick my lazy ass."

"I should have known you're a lost cause."

"No, no I'm not. I got a new spot at the Marriott. I'm doing prep now. No more dishes, old man."

"Lucky for them. They'll save a fortune on breakage."

"I know I could get them to take you on. The union has been great. Everyone I know has caught on somewhere."

This seems to send a cold shadow over Luis. "Aah. Not everyone. So many...gone..."

Manny nods and looks over his shoulder to be sure they are alone keeping his voice very low, "I miss her too. She was such a... well, very special. I know that." He pats Luis on the knee. "It is a terrible thing. I am so sorry."

"Thank you."

Manny feels the silence grow heavier. "Luis. I know how this hurts you. But you must not give up. Forgive me, but you would never allow me to feel so sorry for myself. You know that. You would say to me what I must now say to you. Don't give up on life, my friend. Please."

Luis shakes his head. "I appreciate your love, Manny. I do. But I can't go back to work. Not for them. It's too much."

"No, I'm telling you. The Local will take care of you."

Luis heaves a deep, heavy sigh. "Still buying their mierda, eh?" He shakes his head. "Open your eyes, boy."

"What? You don't really believe what they're saying, do you?"

But the older man's silence tells Manny that he does.

"You're wrong. They didn't start the fire. That's just what the bosses want us to believe. You think they care about us? It's the Local who's looking out for us."

Luis looks at the kid's troubled expression, understands why Manny needs to believe what he does—to survive.

"I don't want to get you in trouble. So just take my word for it. That fire? It was no accident. Believe me."

"You don't... How do you know?"

Luis is silent, but Manny reads a terrible truth in his eyes, realizes there is some secret Luis is holding back.

"You know something, don't you?"

"I know when to keep quiet. I have a family. I have more to lose than a job. Or even a girlfriend. A lot more. Now, please. Leave me alone."

30

Hilton Hotel
Cocktail Lounge

Bartender, Antonio Nogueras, is pouring a slushy boat drink from the blender into a pair of oversized glasses. As he adds a garnish of fresh pineapple, he notices the young woman, alone, walking into the lounge. She looks almost off balance, carrying an enormous briefcase. As she settles wearily onto a barstool, her look says that her bag isn't the only heavy weight she is carrying.

He places the drinks in front of the couple from New Jersey.

"Oh, goodness, Herb. Don't those look delicious?"

Herb regards the little umbrella stabbed into the pineapple slice and plucks it out.

Arching an eyebrow, he looks at the bartender's name tag and asks, "Hey, Antonio? This does have some rum in it, I hope, with all this other fruit and stuff?"

"Call me Tony." He smiles. "A shot of Ronrico dark and one of light. The blend of two rums gives it a nice balance. And on top of that, a shot of Triple sec. Gives it a real kick, my friend." He glances at the man's wife. "But you can hardly taste it." With a slight wisp of innuendo, he adds, "The ladies like it. But they do sneak up on you."

The man gives him a knowing wink and says, "Thanks, Tony."

Tony turns, moving down the bar toward the woman. He remembers her now. She was here with the older gentleman a few nights ago. Attorneys, working on that fire. No wonder she looks like somebody shot her dog.

"Good evening, Miss," he says. "Double martini, wasn't it?"

He knows it was. Twenty-four years behind a bar, Tony's very good at remembering what people drink. A good memory equals good tips.

She looks up at the handsome, silver-haired bartender. "Hello there, Call-Me-Tony. You're right. Only tonight I want something with rum in it. Plenty of rum."

So, he thinks, *she has a good memory too.*

"I can recommend our special, the San Juan Sunset. Pineapple juice, mango juice, coconut, Triple sec, light and dark rum. Everyone seems to like it." He nods back at the couple he just served.

"Not my style, Call-Me-Tony. You have Myers's Rum? Dark?"

"Of course."

"Double shot, with soda. No limes, no pineapples, no coconuts, no cotton candy, no umbrella. Just rum and soda, rocks."

"Good choice," he says.

He puts ice in a highball glass and free-pours a very generous double shot, pulls the soda gun, and tops it with style. As soon as he puts the glass in front of her, Annette takes a long pull.

"Ah," she says. "Perfection. Thank you, Tony."

"Anytime," he says then adds, "I guess it must be hard."

"Hard?" A beat and she gets it. "Oh. The fire. Yeah. Sometimes."

"A terrible tragedy. I don't envy you."

"Today neither do I." She looks at him, reads a sincere look of simpatico in his face, like he's not just chatting up a customer. She asks, "Did you…lose somebody? In the fire?"

He gives a little shrug and says, "Oh, not anyone close, you know. But it's a small world, hospitality. Staff moves around. The hotels hire folks when they're busy, lay them off when it's slow. You get to know faces, you meet people. You know." He shrugs. "But no, thank God. I didn't lose any close friends, nothing like that."

"Glad to hear it." She takes another healthy slug from her drink. "Can I ask you something?"

"Me?" His face seems to close down at this. "I don't really know anything about it. The fire."

She finds his reaction odd, almost defensive. Why did he jump right to that?

"No, of course. I was wondering... You're in the same union too, I assume. The Teamsters?"

"Well, it's not a choice, really. Pretty much the only way to work in one of the big hotels."

"I understand they came to terms. New contract with all the other hotels. Are you guys, the members I mean...do they do a good job for you?"

He looks uncomfortable then says, "I'm not... In what way do you mean?"

"This new contract. You know, pay, bennies, pension, all that stuff? I mean, are you people happy with them?"

At first, he doesn't say anything. But his eyes sweep around the room carefully, and not because he thinks there are thirsty customers waiting. Finally, he gives a rather-hollow smile.

"Look, I'm not into all the politics and stuff. All I know is, it used to be worse. I've been doing this work a long time. Before the Teamsters came in to organize? Those were some bad times, believe me. The hotel people? They took advantage. Squeezed us. And they played things just as rough too. They said the union people were all reds. Which wasn't true, well, not exactly. But politics here? It's different. There's always been a radical element in all the trade unions especially. Socialists. Anarchists. And the whole separatist thing. Some want to make Puerto Rico a state. Some say we should be a country on our own. And all of them? They fight each other, kill people, all the time. It's crazy. So, like I say, I steer clear of all the politics."

Annette has already finished the rum and soda, and she says, "Sure, no. I get it. And the hotel people? When you say they're no angels, I can definitely see what you mean."

"Look, I'm not complaining. You know? I just do my job. That's all."

Annette still wonders about exactly that—her own job, that is.

She pushes her empty glass toward Call-Me-Tony and says, "Why don't we do that again, Tony."

Maybe another double Myers's will chase away the images she can't quite shake: a chain, scorched and blackened; a soot-covered padlock; a charred exit door that couldn't be opened.

"I'll have what she's having." She turns to see Jim slide onto the barstool next to hers. "How much catching up do I have to do?" "Sometimes that's the hardest part of the work," but then he says, "It doesn't always work, trying to pick the good guys from the bad guys. The worse the fire, the more money there is on the line. For all sides. When there's a lot of money on the table? It brings out the worst in everyone."

"I know. I just… The way he defended himself today? Like getting robbed of a little booze could excuse… I mean, that's our client? If you ask me, they killed those people. I can't see past that. I'm sorry, but I can't."

"I can't excuse it either. But I don't try. The one thing I've had to learn? There are no innocent clients."

"No? What about the people who got burned?"

Jim lets that settle. "No, you're right. It is different when you represent the actual victims."

"That's what I'm saying. I don't know if I want to do this."

"I feel the same way. A lot. But…" He tries to think of a way to explain where he thinks they fit into the equation. "This claim, a thing like this fire, it may never go to trial. Probably won't. But either way, the hotel won't get off the hook completely. And they shouldn't. The facts are against us, with the chains on those doors. Or the lack of safety equipment. That stuff helped kill people, and I wouldn't even try to deny it. In fact, that kind of argument would make it worse for them. But at the end of this all, there's going to be a very big pile of chips on the table. And that money in the pot? It'll end up going to all those people who died and their families. Our client? They'll end up putting a lot of those chips into that pot."

"Good. They should."

"Yes. But not all the chips. There wouldn't be anyone dead at all if the Teamsters didn't start that fire. And a lot fewer dead if people didn't put that urethane crap into those cushions that burned. Our job, the only way I can look at this, we're here to make sure a whole lot of the money comes from those other bast—" Jim stops himself. "Excuse me. I don't know what to call them."

"No, *bastards* will do just fine."

"What I mean... Our clients are liable too. And they'll have to pay plenty. But it's up to us to make sure they only pay what's fair. Does that make sense?"

"Honestly? I'm not sure any of it makes sense."

Jim takes another sip of his drink. "I know it would be nice if everything was black and white. But in the real world, the one you talked about? It's not some nice, clean formula in a lab. It's a lot messier." He swirls the ice around in his glass. "The best we can do sometimes is put our thumb on the scale, push it in the right direction. There's never a perfect solution, but we can try to make it better, not worse."

"How do we know which is which?"

"Ask me tomorrow."

"Why? What's tomorrow?"

"Remember those witnesses you wanted to start with? We'll talk to the victims at the hospital."

While Call-Me-Tony keeps Jim and Annette ameliorated during their philosophical musings, another Hilton employee is doing his job, out by the swimming pool. Jorge Cora has been thanked for his service to the union with a new job of his own. Like his former position at the Playa San Juan, Cora is now working for outside services at the Hilton. He is out by the pool now, pushing a rolling bin, picking up used towels that lie discarded wherever the guests fling them when they're done. Once Cora gets them all, he'll add them to the used towels he collects from the container where at least a few of the guests have actually placed their used towels, as they are supposed to do.

Cora doesn't mind that the rich people who stay here don't follow the rules, don't put their towels where they belong. Why should he? If they weren't such slobs, he might not have a job. And he likes his job, especially now, at the Hilton, making an extra buck sixty an hour above what he got at the Playa.

He feels lucky that when the union wanted a couple of reliable members they could count on, they called on Cora and his pal, Fredrico Vázquez. Jorge and Freddy delivered too. They started that fight at the union meeting, just like they were supposed to, set off the melee that drew all the Security Guards. It wasn't their fault the two *pendajos* who were supposed to start a small fire, just to send a message, fucked up royally and burned the fucking place to the ground. That shit's on them, not Cora.

And when Kiko asks Cora to start a little, tiny fire to get that nosy lawyer's attention, that's just what he did. You didn't see Cora burn down the whole fucking place! He did his job and did it right.

It seems weird that he's actually thinking about how Freddy and him got the ball rolling when suddenly that big gorilla steps out from nowhere and taps him on the shoulder. Kiko again, scaring the shit out of him.

But Kiko is all smiles tonight, almost chummy, as he peels off two hundred bucks from a thick roll of twenties.

"For the…message. You did a good job, Jorge."

"Thanks," Cora says, relieved Kiko is smiling, acting all friendly for a change.

But he still feels a loose, cold fear flooding his guts, even when Kiko makes a show of putting away the roll of bills in his pocket then pulling it back out again, like it's an afterthought. He peels off another hundred to Cora's surprise.

"What's this?"

"A little bump. Let you know people appreciate your hard work."

"Really?"

"Right from the top. Mr. Beltran has his eye on you."

Cora nods, glad enough to take the money, but the idea of Mr. Beltran having his eye on Cora doesn't really make him feel all that wonderful.

"So," Kiko says, and Cora thinks, *Oh shit, here it comes. What now?* Kiko puts his meaty paw on Cora's shoulder. "We want to show you that we appreciate your loyalty. We're counting on you."

"Okay... What for?"

"You know, they got you on that list. To go in and get questioned. You do know that, right?"

"Yeah, I was gonna ask about that. I mean, if you want me to say no, I don't have to go."

"No, no. Don't do that. We want you to go. Tell them you want to help, even. But then? Don't tell them shit. Whatever they ask you, you don't know nothing. Right?"

"Sure. No, I get it. I wouldn't say anything. I ain't stupid."

"That's just what I told Mr. Beltran. You're a guy we can count on."

"Damn right. Whatever you want."

"Now that you mention it, there is something else you can help me out with."

Oh, shit, he thinks. *Now what?*

"Of course, anything."

"I been trying to find your buddy. Vázquez? Know where he is?"

"Freddy?" Cora feels a tingle of fear at the back of his neck. "He's at the Marriott now. Isn't he? That's what I heard. You guys got him juiced in at Marriott, right?"

"We did. But he ain't ever showed up for work."

"Really? That's... It ain't like Freddy. He's a good man."

"So you know where he is?"

"Me..." Kiko just keeps drilling him with those dead shark eyes, and he can't manage to keep himself quiet. "I don't... It's not like we hang or anything. I could give you his phone number if—"

"He ain't answering. He don't seem to be home because I been by there a few times. Freddy don't seem to be around no place."

"I don't...no, really, I got no idea. Why would he..."

"You know, those people you're gonna talk to? They got him on the list too. But when I go to see him about what to say, I find he's not around. Makes me worry. What's he hiding for?"

"Hiding? No, I don't think… Look, Freddy? He's a standup guy. Really, you don't need to worry. He's no rat. I know him. He's okay."

Kiko isn't smiling now. "Oh…you know him good then? 'Cause I thought you said you don't hang with him or nothing."

"No, right, I don't. I mean, just from work I know him. And from, you know, when we did that thing for you, at the meeting. But I don't…" Cora trails off, his throat going all dry now, too scratchy to talk.

"Okay, Jorge. I believe you."

"Sure, of course. If I knew anything…"

"You'll tell me. Right? If you hear from Freddy?"

"Yeah, yeah. No problem. I'll keep… I mean, you know, if—"

The lightning bolt of pain when Kiko squeezes his shoulder, right up near his neck, it almost buckles Cora to his knees. That big, hard thumb digging into some nerve, unbelievable how bad it hurts.

"I know you will, Jorge. I'm counting on you. And I know when you talk to them people, you're gonna do the right thing."

31

Hospital Burn Ward
San Juan

As THEY MOVE from bed to bed, patient to patient, Annette is glad that Jim didn't listen to her that first day. If she had to do this, had to see these people right off the bat like that? She might have been on the next plane out.

The burn victims are rough, to be expected, but still. There is knowing, and then there is seeing. When they get to the hospital, the head nurse, Gloria Reynoso, intercepts them before they can enter her burn ward. Yes, yes, she says, she understands how important it is to interview these victims and all that. But she insists the proper protocols must be followed to maintain a sterile unit. She puts them through a rigorous process of scrubbing and disinfecting, makes them change into clean scrubs, even put on little booties.

"I know I am a pain in the ass, everyone says that," she grumbles as she checks them out from head to foot. "But I am the one responsible."

"Yes, ma'am," Jim avows. "I practically know the drill by heart. I've been in far too many burn wards."

"Oh? Well, good, then you understand." But that doesn't mean Gloria isn't going to make sure she's understood. She doesn't cut down on her lecturing, just directs it all toward Annette now. "There's more than enough reason for me to worry," she prattles. "Are you aware that patients who are badly burned are more likely to die of infections of their open wounds than to die from the fire's actual tissue damage?"

Annette looks at Jim, who nods. "Oh. Well, I want to do whatever you feel is necessary."

"So. Put these on," Gloria interrupts, handing them surgical masks.

"No problem," Annette says through the mask she puts on. "Is there anything else we—"

"And wear these." She hands them both a pair of latex gloves and watches them intently until they are fully gloved.

The hospital interviews are shorter than the depositions they take in their office, much less formal, with the boilerplate stuff cut to the bone. Jim asks the questions mostly. Annette runs the small recorder, and after each interview, she pops out the mini cassette and replaces it with a new one.

More difficult for Annette, both technically and emotionally, are their interviews with the patients who are suffering the effects of inhaling the toxic gasses from the burning urethane cushions. Having to hear their painful, croaking gags sends her mind drifting back to when she was in eighth grade.

Annette gets home from school, puts her book bag down on the dining-room table, and pulls out her math homework. She carries it into her parents' bedroom and relieves her Aunt Lois. On school days, Lois sits at the side of her brother, Annette's dad, tending to him until Annette gets home, and takes over the caregiver role. Lois always fills her in on the day's activity journal, listing date, time, and every med, every intake of food or water, every urination or defecation, even changes of position to avoid bedsores. Lois also goes over it verbally in painstaking detail, even as Annette is reading it all in her aunt's cramped scrawl.

There are fewer entries now than two months ago. Those days, back when her dad first got home to begin his hospice, there was much more to do: treating his terrible cough symptoms, helping him to the bathroom (when he could still make that trip), trying to feed him the few things he could stand to swallow or tolerate without vomiting. After that last futile round of chemo fails to even slow down the cancer ravaging his lungs, they take him home to die. He's still sick from the treatments at first and vomits anything he swallows. It seems impossible that this man, all skin and skeleton, can lose even more weight. He does, though, and then another change over the next three weeks. As the effect of the chemo toxins wear off, there are days he actually seems to improve. He even gets back some appetite, not enough to replace any of the vanished flesh but at least a hint of color returns to the hollow cheeks, the sunken eye sockets. But this is a false hope, of course, and it doesn't last. After a month, the hunger of that wolf eating his lungs from within is the only appetite remaining inside her father.

The caretaking is easier now. It consists mainly of providing the generous doses of sublingual morphine. There is hardly any of the wheezing struggle for breath or the racking spasms of coughing. Now her dad is mostly asleep. She hopes he dreams of the days when he taught her to fish, when they hiked for miles and miles to reach some frigid lake and spent the hours shivering so much their poles would shake, or the time he taught her to ride a bike, or when they went ice-skating…

She is terrified each day now, praying he will not die until her mother gets home from work at eight in the evening. But she is relieved, especially for him, that his active suffering stage is pretty much over. All of them wait patiently for Death's arrival. But the old trickster, the boney shade who can never be avoided, can also never be rushed. He will come only when he decides the hour is right, come in his own good time, not before, not after. Annette sits by the shell of her dying father, doing her best to concentrate on her algebra and not listen to the irregular rattle of his stubborn, hopeless breaths.

Hearing the awful wheezes and terrible coughing in the hospital burn ward is hard on Annette. She has to stay close by too, holding the recorder, trying to capture the misty, insubstantial words as the victims struggle to answer Jim's questions. As he goes through his inquiries, though, she sees a different side to him, a kindness that comes through no matter how terrible the questions are, how painful the answers. This patience, this gentleness, shows her a side of Jim that it seems he must check at the door of the office, or even during their meals together or their rambling conversations at the bar in the evenings. She knows this is a very private part of him she is seeing now, the loving part that he saves for his wife and his girls; but somehow, the suffering of these witnesses coaxes it out of him.

They break her heart too, every one of them, to see an otherwise perfectly healthy young mother, fit and shapely, croaking out answers in the raspy voice of a four-packs-a-day baritone; to see a father whose overdeveloped right forearm is the sure sign of an avid tennis player, wheezing and coughing, as some neurological damage has his left hand curled and trembling.

Among the burn victims, she nearly breaks down listening to a twenty-three-year-old security guard, one of the unselfish platoon of private cops that were under the command of Captain Delgado. The burns over most of his chest and arms are healing; although it will take many skin grafts before he can leave the hospital. He will not be returning to his watch, however. Glass shards from an exploding window have taken his sight. He won't be watching anything ever again.

For most of the morning, it feels like a cruel and pointless intrusion to be questioning these broken souls. So many stories sound the same. She is hardly listening when she notices Jim's attention perk up.

"What?" he says. "I'm sorry, can you say a little more about that?"

Annette leans in, holding the recorder closer to the woman. Francesca Perez is one of the housekeeping staff who was lucky enough to get out of the guest-room section of the hotel with relatively minor burns and lung damage.

"The first fire, I mean." she repeats. "Not the big one. The first one, in the linen closet. Are you looking into that one too?"

"You mean, there was a fire inside the hotel? Where the rooms are?"

"Yes, yes. The linen closet on the fourth floor?"

"Was this before or during the big fire."

"Oh, yes, yes, before. Two weeks before."

Jim and Annette exchange a significant look, then Jim asks, "Did you see that fire?"

"Me? No, I didn't work that day. It was, oh, I guess…it was three days before Christmas. Yes, I remember that day. I did some Christmas shopping. Mostly for my kids. I never know what to get for my husband."

"But, about the fire…"

"The first fire? I guess it wasn't much, really. It still smelled a little smoky when I came back on the next day. It didn't really do damage, hardly. They had to throw away a bunch of sheets and towels, is all. Because of the smell."

"Do you know how this fire started? Was it accidental?"

"Oh, no, no way. It was somebody lit a can of Sterno inside the closet. That's what I heard from Meredith. She's the one found the fire."

"Meredith? Can you give us a last name? We'd like to speak with her."

"Her name was Meredith Martinez."

"Was?"

"So terrible, how she died. And her poor husband, Hector? He got terribly burned himself. You should talk to him. I know Meredith. She told him everything, all the time. I know she told him all about that fire A nice woman, but she, you know the kind, she never shut up about nothing."

"So, this Hector Martinez. You say he survived?" Jim's eyes are alive with the sharp focus of a hunter.

"Yes, yes. He's right here. In the hospital."

Annette gets up, hands the recorder to Jim. "I'll go check at the nurse's station, find where he is. Be right back."

"You don't have to hurry off," says Francesca. "He's at Physical Therapy. I saw, they took him down there about an hour ago. He should be back any minute."

Jim shuts off the recorder, hands it back to Annette. "I think we should find him right now." He turns to Francesca, quickly saying, "Thanks very much. You've been a big help."

But before they can turn away and hurry off, the woman is waving her hand and pointing. "See there? I told you. Here he comes now."

A man in a wheelchair is being rolled off the elevator. He wears a glum stare, a hopeless look, maybe because his hands have been burned so badly. His fingers are barely stubs—bad enough for anyone, only Hector Martinez was the Playa San Juan Casino's best blackjack dealer.

"Thanks again, you've been a big help," Annette tells Francesca, turning to follow Jim.

He is already up, hurrying toward Hector, making his way across the ward of fire victims. Annette is on her feet now, in hot pursuit, when the air is shredded by the near deafening scream of the klaxon.

"What's that?" Annette practically has to shout as patients all over the ward begin to panic, screaming in terror at a blaring horn, repeating short bursts.

Jim gets it, and he knows why the people around them are shrieking with such traumatized horror. Of course, they would.

"Oh dear god," he realizes. "That's the fire alarm!"

32

Interview Room
Crystal Towers Office Plaza

THERE WAS NO actual fire.

Mike Peralta is here, telling them the bomb threat was phoned in, but no bomb. His team thoroughly went over the entire hospital, along with bomb experts from ATF. It appears the bomb threat called in was a fake, meant to put the fear of God in the witnesses who were being interviewed.

"And, I suppose, in you guys too," he adds.

Like that's going to happen, says the withering look he gets from Jim.

"We've already set up a return visit," says Jim. "I just hope we can still get some decent interviews done. Damn Teamsters."

Mike looks from Jim over to Annette. "Look, I don't have to tell you to watch yourselves. I'm going to detail some surveillance to keep an eye on you two. Especially around the Hilton. I don't like that you're basically living in a nest of Teamsters there."

"We could change hotels, but it won't be any different. Will it?" Annette points out. "That would just make it look like we're scared of them."

Mike is good at reading faces, knows how to pick out all the little tells that reveal when a person is trying to bluff their way past fear. Annette's face tells him she really does believe she can take care of herself. Brave woman. Naive. But she has guts, at least, give her credit for that.

"Mike, I'll keep an eye out," Jim assures him. "Really, I'm fully aware of what those thugs are capable of. But I doubt they'd come directly at us and tip their hand that way. We'll be fine."

Mike shrugs, and nods. "Just be careful, that's all I'm saying."

"Speaking of the Lucifers of labor," Annette puts in, "we have some real doozies on deck for today. Should we get started?"

"Who's up first?" Jim asks, getting settled in his chair.

Questioning Kiko Cabrera is kind of like discussing Descartes with a Rottweiler. *Maybe we'd get more out of him if I threw in a few pieces of raw meat,* Annette thinks. They've heard *"I don't remember"* more times than a week spent in an Alzheimer's ward, especially with regard to anything that happened on the day of the fire. Kiko claims a hotel security guard hit him over the head with a riot baton. *Really?* she thinks. *Was he standing on a ladder so he could reach that high?* She stifles a laugh, imagining what Jim would say to her if she had actually asked that. But she doesn't because this human pile driver has already mentioned he is considering a personal injury suit against their client, the hotel. Kiko alleges his tort-worthy concussion has left him with no memory whatsoever of the union meeting, the riot that followed, or of the fire itself. The whole day is all a blank, he claims.

Roberto Beltran arrives with the attorney for Local 901, Aurelio Feliciano, in tow. Other than stipulating to such boilerplate as name, rank, and serial number, Feliciano stops every question cold with the usual dodgy mumbo jumbo. When Jim points out this is a deposition, not a trial, and says Beltran has to answer, all they get is another litany of lost memory. The interview is a waste of time, and the transcript a waste of paper.

The next subject to tap dance through their questions is Jorge Cora. He admits he attended the union meeting. No, he has no idea why a fight broke out, didn't see it. He was just listening to Beltran and Feliciano talk about the status of negotiations when out of nowhere someone punched him, and all of a sudden, he was caught in a brawl. He tells them he doesn't even know much about the areas involved in the fire. He's was in outdoor services. He never really had any reason to go inside the hotel or the casino.

Nobody asks him where he works now, and he sure as shit doesn't volunteer that now he works around the swimming pool at the Hilton. The fact that he avoids any eye contact with Jim doesn't clue them to anything. Most of the other Teamster hotel workers never meet his eyes either.

But the interview ends without touching on his work at the Hilton (and thank God, nothing about the pool, where Cora started a fire that night while Jim was swimming). Cora leaves the room with his pulse pounding in his throat and his stomach flipping. In fact, he's lucky he makes it to the men's washroom in time. When he is finished vomiting, he spends five minutes just getting his breath to slow down to normal again.

He splashes water on his face and walks quickly through the open office area to the elevator. He gets inside and finally feels his pounding heart begin to slow down as the glass elevator car carries him down to ground level. He thinks about making a thumbs-up sign, but he's afraid his hand will tremble if he tries it.

The next witness on the list is a no-show, Federico Vázquez.

"What's his story?" Jim asks Martin Flores, one of the interview staffers sitting in today.

"So far, nobody's been able to contact him. I'm sorry, we should have taken him off the list until we can set up a schedule."

"Never mind," Jim says. "Any luck catching up with this guy Rosa yet? He's the one who was rounding up members to go to that meeting. I'd really like to ask him why he never showed up there himself."

"He's another one we're still looking for."

Jim nods, exchanging a look with Mike Peralta. Mike gives a little nod. He'll get some people on it too.

"Okay," Jim says, "let's see the next one."

As Wilfredo Torres limps into the room, he has a sneer on his face, doing his best to look like a tough guy. It's hard to sell, though, seeing as he's got a cast on his right arm going from his wrist practically all the way up to his shoulder. His face is puffy and swollen, and there are stitches in his chin and jaw. The black eyes Torres sports are just turning a hideous shade of greenish purple. A groan escapes him when he sits down in the hot seat, suggesting back pain.

Jim wants to hear him say, *"You should see the other guy,"* but knows that isn't going to happen. In fact, Torres does his best to say as little as Kiko. And, like Kiko, the only subject Torres feels willing to discuss is the claim that his injuries, too, came as a result of the overzealous attempts at crowd control meted out by Delgado's security force. His assertions sound even less convincing than the big gorilla was earlier. Other than that, it's like pulling teeth even getting him to confirm that he was a building engineer. Only he slips up, with a touch of pride, admitting modestly that yes, he did have a supervisory role in that capacity.

"So," Jim probes, "you had access to pretty much every part of the property. For maintenance purposes, correct?"

"I guess."

"Including areas not open to the public. Is that right?"

"If you say so," Torres says, trying to look bored.

"Well, what I am asking is for you to say so. Can you confirm you had access to public and nonpublic areas of the hotel, yes or no?"

"Of course. You know I did. And I had fourteen other guys on my staff had the same thing. How the hell else could we do our job?"

"Did all of your men have keys to open any area that was locked?"

"Mostly. Well, they had keys to get in where they needed to go. But you know, it depends. The guys who did plumbing, they had their keys. The HVAC guys had theirs, the electricians, you know. They had what they needed."

"And if they didn't have the right key? Who would they come to?"

"They had what they need. I said that."

"Okay. So how about you?"

"What about me?"

"If they didn't have the right key, you're the supervisor, so you had a lot of responsibility, right? I mean, unless you weren't really in charge."

"That's bullshit. I ran that whole department."

"Okay, noted. So they would come to you?"

"I told you. They didn't have to."

"I understand. But my point is, if they needed a key they didn't have, they could always get it from you, isn't that right?"

"Like I told you, that never happens (happened)."

"But still, you did have the keys to open any lock on the property. Isn't that right?"

"What's the difference? Sure. Somebody had to, right? And that's me, the guy in charge. Okay?"

"Did you have keys to open the locks to the upper ballroom?"

Now Jim sees a flash of anger followed by a jolt of fear. Bingo. Torres has to take a moment to weigh his answer.

"I get it, what you're asking. Yeah, I'm one of the people who had keys to that place."

"So, you could go into the upper ballroom at any time. Correct?"

Torres tries to go all cagey now. "Yeah. So? Just about everybody did. It's a big space, lots of systems in there. Most of my guys had keys to it because they all had things they needed to work on. Plumbing, electric, all the mechanics. If you want, I can give you a list of everyone who could open that building. Is that what you're after?"

"That would be helpful, yes."

But it would have been more helpful, Jim thinks, if the key questions had narrowed things down a little.

They move on.

When they finally finish with Torres, he feels a clammy sweat run down between his shoulder blades. His armpits feel like they're soaked, and the sweat is making his goddamn cast itch like hell. His back hurts now, worse than usual, has to be from the tension. He feels like he was all tied up in knots in there. He goes over and over what he said. He gave them nothing, nothing much anyway, not really, only stuff they would know anyway, right?

Only he knows Kiko is going to grill him on every damn thing, the he-said she-said bullshit, over and over. Goddamnit, he should have laid low, like Rosa's doing. This was fucked.

When he gets in the glass elevator, and the transparent car starts to descend, he puts on what he hopes is a confident face; and with his good arm, he gives a vigorous thumbs-up.

The office building across the street from the Crystal Towers Office Plaza has few tenants. It's at least three-quarters unoccupied, in fact. It, too, is a modern-looking design, mostly steel and glass. To cut down on the heat of the sun, all the window glass has a highly reflective treatment, so the whole place looks like it's made of mirrors. You can't really see into the interior of the building at all.

But from inside you can easily see out.

The second-floor room has a perfect view of the Crystal Towers Office Plaza. Directly across Calle Mille Flores, it's an open view of the glass elevator towers. This is why Local 901 rents the place, the day after Jim's investigators leased their offices. They can see every witness who goes in or out of the law office across the street. Everyone who rides up or down in that glass elevator.

In fact, the high-resolution, professional-grade video camera trained on the elevator is able to record an excellent image of every person going in or out of the investigator's suite, especially with the special telephoto zoom lens on the camera, which can provide not just a close up of anyone's face in that elevator; it can get so close you could count the hairs on their eyebrows.

And at the end of each day, a videotape of who is coming and going is delivered to Local 901's office, where Teamster President Ricardo Beltran can review every single face and identify every person who is interviewed; can put together a list of all the people who might betray him.

And then he can go over the list with Kiko and decide what to do about it.

33

Hilton Hotel
Cocktail Lounge

JIM AND ANNETTE return to the hotel after a long, frustrating day of interviewing people who don't want to talk to them. They are headed for the elevators when Annette slows down, looking to the left, into the bar.

"Know what? I'm going to grab a drink."

"After today? I'll buy."

Call-Me-Tony sees them coming, and by the time they park themselves on two barstools, he's already in front of them.

"What kind of day is this? Martini day or rum day?"

"Eh," she says, holding out a flat hand, rocking it in a classic so-so gesture, and turning to Jim. "What do you say?"

"It wasn't great. But it wasn't terrible. Martini?"

Annette gives a single nod. "Hear that, Tony? And very dry."

"Is there another kind?" He produces two martini glasses with a flourish. Into each he pours a small splash of vermouth, swirls it around to wet the sides, and then dumps it out into the sink. Then he fills both with Bombay gin and sticks an olive in each. "My Sahara Special. They don't come any drier."

They each raise their glass to Tony and then clink them lightly.

"To weasel words," proposes Jim.

"And circumlocution," Annette adds.

After his first sip, Jim says, "Tony, you're a gentleman and a scholar."

"Sir, I'm glad for you both this wasn't a rum day."

He moves off as a waitress brings a drink order from the dining room.

"You had Mr. Engineering Supervisor going for a while there, Boss."

"Torres? Yeah. Couldn't land the fish though."

"Still, I learn just watching you. The way you worked his puffed-up ego? Made him want to brag how important he was, the king of the keys and all. It was sweet."

"Yeah, but he twigged where I was trying to lead him. Very well coached, I have to say."

"You think he was telling the truth, though? That a lot of his people have a key to that ballroom?"

"Who knows?" But he smiles. "We can sure follow up with the rest of the *engineers*, though. He's probably lying. That would narrow it down some."

"I think he's one of those picture-worth-a-thousand-word deals. He didn't get the crap beat out of him like that by Delgado's men."

"I wondered if you'd noticed that. What happened to the poor guy anyway? Did he maybe walk into a wall?"

"Me? I kinda like Kiko for that," she opines. "Somebody serious, anyway."

"No shortage of candidates. Teamsters could open up a separate Local just for arm-breakers."

"I'm curious about that guy who didn't show. Rosa?" She sips her drink, speculative. "Wouldn't it be interesting if he looked like somebody ran him through the spanking machine too…"

Jim likes that idea. "You have a very suspicious mind."

"I'm learning from the master." She thinks a moment and looks down the bar, her gaze resting on Call-Me-Tony.

Jim notices this and says, "What's with the look? You haven't even half-finished that Sahara Special yet."

"Do you ever get used to it? Having people lie to you, hold back on you?"

"Occupational hazard, young lady."

"I mean, it's one thing if they're on the hot seat in that room of ours…"

"Must be the way I go around with that rubber hose." But Annette is still looking at Call-Me-Tony, and Jim has to ask her, "What's with the look? He didn't even work at the Playa."

"Right." She swigs down the rest of her martini. "So I gotta wonder… Why did he get so antsy when I brought up the fire with him? I didn't think much about it, not at the time. But he went all around the mulberry bush to convince me he keeps his nose out of union business. I wonder why that is?"

She catches Call-Me-Tony's eye and holds up her empty glass.

He comes over with a smile. "That was quick."

"Maybe today was worse than we let on," she says. Jim sits back, listens carefully, lets Annette play whatever angle she's got on her mind.

"Sorry to hear that," he says. "So. Another one then?"

"I bet you know what it's like, listening to people lie their ass off right to your face. You must hear all kinds of stuff in here."

Jim sees it too now, the way Call-Me-Tony shuts down at this.

When he answers Annette, his tone is all chilly, "I don't… what are you suggesting? That I eavesdrop on people?"

"I don't know. Do you?"

It's deliberately insulting, the way she says it. A thing like that would make a man angry, Jim thinks, especially a man of Tony's toxic macho generation. But it's not anger he sees on Tony's face. It's stone-cold fear.

"Tony," Jim dips in, "my young friend doesn't mean to hurt your feelings. But she has a point. Let me ask you. Do you know a guy named Rosa? Or maybe Kiko? They're Teamsters."

"Like I said to her, we're all Teamsters, whether we like it or not. If we want to work, that's how it is."

"Have you ever met Roberto Beltran? You know who he is, right?"

"Everybody does."

"Has he ever come in here? You'd remember that."

"What of it? All kinds of people come in here for a drink. Just like you. It's a nice place."

"So does Beltran come in here? Kiko? Rosa? Or a guy named Torres, do you know him?"

"I have no idea what you're getting at, sir. But I wish you would leave me out of this, or do your drinking somewhere else." Tony turns, walking away.

Jim and Annette both notice, though, that Tony is looking all around the bar and scanning the dining room, as if he wants to be sure no one could mistake him for a guy who talks too much to the wrong people.

34

Hospital Burn Ward
San Juan

GLORIA KNOWS THEY'RE coming and is at the elevator to meet them. She lays right into it. They upset her patients. That bomb thing, it freaked them out. She asks why they can't wait, at least let these people heal up some before they start scaring them all over again.

"Okay, for now," Jim says. "But there is one patient we need to talk to."

"Hector Martinez?" adds Annette.

Gloria's brow furrows. "Oh. But he's not here."

"PT again?" Jim asks. "We can see him down there."

"No, I mean not here. At the hospital. He was transferred to a private clinic that specializes in burns." She reaches into a pocket, feeling around.

A quick look between Jim and Annette. "Where is this place?"

Gloria pulls a business card from her pocket and hands it to Jim.

When Jim calls the number, it's as bad as he feared. There is no such place. Somebody took Hector for a little outing.

Jim and Annette get into their car, pulling away from the hospital parking lot. As they turn onto the street, another car pulls out, following them.

"Have a guess about what's going on?" Annette starts.

182

"Hector? Somebody doesn't want us talking to him, obviously, which tells us Hector knows who started that first fire in the closet. It has to be connected."

"Dry run, you think?"

"Not exactly. More like an opening bid, that's my guess. Start small, see if the hotel people get the message and play ball on the contract."

"I guess they needed more convincing."

"And now the Local has an experienced firebug on staff."

"Experienced, maybe, but no expert. I don't think they meant for that fire to spread like that, do you?"

Jim is listening, but looks a little distracted. "I tend to agree. Talk that through."

Annette goes through her logic, "It wouldn't get what they're after. They want to scare the hotel into giving them a better contract. If they burn the place to the ground, there is no contract. And they have what, a thousand members out of work? No. That doesn't help them. It would be stupid."

"That makes good sense. And those bastards might be ruthless, but they're not stupid." Jim's eyes flick over to check the rearview mirror again. "There's nothing they won't do to help themselves. But they wouldn't cut off their nose to spite their face. No, you're right. That fire was supposed to be big enough to scare all the hotels. But somebody screwed up, and it got way out of control."

Annette thinks about all those people back in the burn ward and all those others. "Screwed up? I'd say so."

As they turn another corner, Jim checks the rearview mirror, and now he sure he's right. Annette picks up on Jim's eyeline and starts to turn around to look behind them.

"No," he says. "Don't turn around."

Which only confirms her suspicion.

"They're following us. Right?"

"Somebody is. Not very good at it either."

"So? You can probably lose them, right?"

"That's one approach…" But she can see he's considering their options. "When we park the car, just follow my lead, okay?"

They drive the speed limit, as if they're ignorant of the car staying on their tail. Jim turns onto Calle Mille Flores, two blocks from the Crystal Towers Office Plaza. The other car turns, following behind them. When they reach their building, Jim turns into the parking lot and pulls into the spot marked with their names on it. As they get out of the car, Jim watches the follow car cruise slowly past.

"Well," he says, "they know we're home safe. Let's go inside."

"You think they're gone?"

"Hell no."

As Jim starts to stroll from the parking lot, around to the front entrance, Annette goes along.

"Just try to look natural," she mutters, lips hardly moving.

Her sarcasm almost makes Jim laugh out loud. As they get right near the front door, he stops, acting out a *what-did-I-forget* little pantomime, patting pockets with a puzzled look.

Under his breath, he tells Annette, "Look in your ridiculous saddlebag there for me, okay?"

She opens her huge attaché to root around in. "What do you need?"

"Only about twenty seconds. Wherever he parked, he might be trying to catch up now." He waits another moment. "Okay, that should do. Let's go inside."

As soon as the get in, Jim takes her elbow and pulls her into a little nook by the door. They wait quietly for a few moments.

The lobby door opens, and just as a man walks in, Jim lunges and grabs for him. Annette is impressed how fast her boss moves, like a blur. He has the man's arm in a hammer lock before she can blink.

"Ow! Hey, easy!" the man yelps.

"Hello there, Call-Me-Tony." She enjoys the surprised look on Jim's face as he lets go and takes a look at the man he grabbed from behind.

"Jesus," says Tony. He shrugs to check if his arms still work. "Well, I guess this is going to be a rum day then, huh?"

"Why are you following us, Tony?"

"I'm not going to start asking around where your office is."

"And…you didn't want to talk at the hotel?"

He answers Annette with a nod, "I didn't know you were going to that hospital first. But I just stuck with you."

Jim nods. "I understand your caution. I assume that means there's something you've decided to tell us?"

The three of them set out for the fifth-floor suite, in the glass elevator, of course.

As they settle into the interview room, Tony quails as he sees Annette take out her mini tape recorder.

"Hey, woah. What's that?"

"Oh, this? It's my little magic box. It snatches words right out of the air, and later it helps me remember them. Be careful though. It might try to capture your soul."

"Are you saying you are not willing to be recorded?" Jim asks.

"Damn right, I'm not."

Jim nods to Annette, and she puts the recorder away.

"All right then. Off the record. What's on your mind, Tony?"

"Okay. So, you were right. I did hear some guys a couple weeks before Christmas. They were in a booth. So I only heard part of what they talked about."

"Do you know who they were?"

"No comment."

"That's a big help, Call-Me-Tony'," Annette says flatly. "What am I gonna call these mysterious bar patrons?"

"I'm not giving up any names. And you didn't hear this from me."

"I don't hear anything at all so far," Annette pokes. Jim gives her a look. "I'm sorry. I understand your caution. Can you say if they were Teamsters?"

"Of course. What else? Just no names."

"That's fine. This is in total confidence," Jim assures him again. "If you'd feel better, give Annette a dollar. Then we can say you retained us as your lawyers, and cloak everything you say with the privilege."

"That's okay. I trust you not to let out you heard it from me." He swallows, trying to get enough spit to let his tongue move.

Annette jumps up, grabbing a bottled water from a credenza along the wall. She pretends to wipe the table in front of him, like it's a bar, and puts the water in front of Tony.

"Will that be all, sir?"

Tony laughs, relaxes just a touch. "Thanks, bartender."

He takes a long drink of water, and she sits back down.

"So this is back about three weeks before the…new year. There's about six of them. I can tell they're talking about the negotiations. And they…" He stops himself.

"Never mind who, that's okay for now," Jim says, all calm and brimming with reassurance. "Just give us the gist of the conversation, okay?"

"I hear them say the hotel name, you know, Playa San Juan. So I know that's about the contract. Because it's Playa's turn in the barrel this year. Everyone knows that. Anyway, something they tried, I didn't hear what it was, but if was a real screwup. It didn't work. So they're going to have to raise the ante on New Year's Eve day because they are going to walk out on strike at midnight. So they want to give a little leverage to it when they do it. They decide to call a union meeting, get all the staff they can together. And while there's just a skeleton staff on duty, that's when they'll do it."

"Did you hear what, specifically, they planned to do?" Jim probes, giving him some space.

Tony takes another sip of water. "I… You know, I couldn't hear everything exactly. I mean… Look, I can't be sure just what—"

Annette cuts in, bad cop, "Did they say they were starting a fire, Tony? Or not?"

"Hey, hey. Let him tell it." Jim smiles at Tony. "Sorry about that. Take your time. That's fine."

"Look, at the time? I didn't hear them say it was going to be a fire. If I heard that, I would have… I didn't know. Really. Not about it being a fire. I just knew… They said they would make some big distraction, and then when everyone was out of the way, you know, like misdirection? And then they would pull something to really get the hotel's attention."

"And you don't feel you can…give us any names? Even a rough idea? It would really help us out."

"No. I mean it. No names."

"I understand."

"You know what they do when they think you're a rat?"

"That's your decision, Tony. I'm not trying to push you."

"Well, don't. I can't say any more. I just… I didn't know it would be a fire like that. I swear. I would have said something…" And he (snuff) is starting to choke on the past now. "All those… I knew people, you know? I…I'd say something, I mean…"

He is really struggling not to let tears get the better of him. They back off, just let him sit with his face in his hands, trying to keep it together.

"It's okay, Tony," Annette says softly. No more bad cop anymore. "Thanks for coming to us. If there's anything else, anytime you feel comfortable, you can tell us. Up to you."

"Don't talk to me at the bar anymore. At all, okay?" He tries to swallow the fear in his throat. "I mean it. Just order and don't start up with…anything."

There is a soft rap on the door—unusual because the staff knows better than to interrupt the flow of an interview. So it must be something important, Jim knows, and he goes to the door and opens it a crack, listens, turns back inside, and closes the door firmly.

He gives Annette a serious look and says, "Tony, thanks very much. I know that was hard for you. We appreciate you took a chance to help us out." He turns to meet Annette's worried stare. "We have to leave right now, Tony. If you want to take some time for yourself, feel free. Long as you need."

And with a sharp jerk of Jim's head, Annette is up on her feet. She hurries to follow Jim, who's already out the door.

"Thanks, Tony," she says as she passes him without slowing down.

35

Alley—Commercial Zone
San Juan

MIKE PERALTA WAVES to them as he sees Jim and Annette round the corner and start down the alley toward him. He stands by a dented dumpster, trying to ignore the buzzing squadron of flies. A forensic team is just setting up to go to work on the crime scene.

"Thanks," Mike says. "I thought you better know about this right away, but you didn't need to come down here."

"When did you find the body?"

"Right before I called you."

Jim reaches the dumpster and takes a peek inside, sees exactly what he expects, and pulls back.

"It looks like things have kicked up a notch." As Annette steps forward, he puts a hand up. "You don't want to see this."

"Oh, stop with that." She brushes past the men and peers down into the dumpster, at the thing in there drawing all the flies. She doesn't look away though. "Wow, that's harsh. What did that to his face? Was it a shotgun?"

Mike doesn't seem to notice her questions. He's still puzzling over her unwavering stare at the corpse. He gives Jim a look, his expression says, *What the hell is with this woman?* Jim gestures with open hands, *Don't ask me.*

Annette studies the body without so much as blinking, taking in details, analyzing what she can see. She tilts her head, focusing her attention on the shredded face of the victim.

Without turning from it, she says, "Crap. I left my camera at the office. You have one in the car, Jim?"

"Sorry."

"So, Mike? Shotgun, right?" asking again, since he didn't answer.

"Looks that way."

"Must have been close range too. I bet they don't want to make it easy to identify this body, right?"

"That's my working hypothesis, yeah."

"So you know who this guy is yet?"

"Not a clue so far."

Something else catches her forensically curious eye. "Oh, man. Are those powder burns?"

"Probably. But there are burns all over the body. Not fresh either. Bandaged. One of your witnesses, I'm guessing. Hard to say which yet."

"Wonder if running his prints will help," she mutters.

"Who knows if they're even on file," Jim says.

"Wouldn't matter, really. We can't run fingerprints on this guy."

The instant he hears this, Jim's face falls.

"Don't tell me," he says. "He doesn't have fingers. They're burned off."

"How did you know?"

36

Cocktail Lounge
Hilton Hotel

MIKE PERALTA SITS in a booth with Jim and Annette, trying to argue them into something and hitting a brick wall.

"Please. You're not taking this seriously enough."

"Mike, listen," Jim says. "You can't say we didn't expect this."

"Murdering witnesses? No, I expect it. I expect it's not over either. That's my point."

"But Mike, we're not witnesses," Annette says calmly, trying to catch the eye of the waitress.

"You're a threat. That's all it takes."

"It's different, Mike. You kill a witness, they're gone. Problem solved. You start killing investigators, all you get is more investigators."

"Oh, really? Then why did they try to kill you in Las Vegas?"

Jim sees Annette's head snap back around at this, staring at him. "Who did? The Teamsters?"

Jim gives a quick nod. "That was differ—"

"Why didn't you tell me about that?"

"He should have," Mike grumbles. "He should have told me too. I only found out when my people started looking at prior suspected Teamster hits."

"That was a completely different set of circumstances," Jim starts. But then he stops and changes tracks. "But... No, I should have...have said something to you... I'm sorry. Honestly, I didn't think… I've been a lot more careful. Not getting all up in their face, the way I did back then. I let myself get frustrated there, I admit. I started pushing too hard, and…"

"And getting too close," Mike says. "It's not your technique that's the issue. It's the result. You get close enough to prove it, they go to extremes."

"Which just shows we're getting somewhere," Annette throws in, but she is turned to the waitress who has finally arrived. "Rum and soda. Myers's. Double. No lemons, no limes, no fruits of any kind." She turns to the men. "Fellas? This counts as a rum day for me. What say you?"

"What she said." Jim nods.

"I'll have a Heineken," Mike says, wanting the waitress gone so he can raise the urgency of his pitch. "Listen to me, Jim. I don't care whether you think you can handle yourself. Maybe you can. But I don't see why you should make it any easier for them to take a run at you." Then he looks at Annette and adds this kicker, "And what about your protégé here? How will you feel if something happens to her?"

"Oh, don't worry about that, Mike," she pipes in. "I'm sure they'd kill Jim first, so it won't bother him when they kill me."

"See?" Mike says, turning back on Jim. "That's what I'm worried about. This one. She doesn't know enough to take this seriously."

"Oh, come on, Mike," she says. "You already have those two guys in the Impala dogging us."

Mike is surprised. "Wha—You made them?"

"Seriously? Crew cuts, dark glasses, crappy suits? I assumed the whole idea was to make it obvious to anyone that we had an FBI detail watching us. Like a visible deterrent."

"She's very observant," Jim tosses in.

"So I see. Look, I'm not trying to scare you. Not that it would do any good. But at least, let's do something about your most vulnerable situation."

"Which is?" Jim asks.

"This is. This place. You know everybody working at the Hilton is a Teamster. Any one of them could come at you a hundred different ways."

"But like we said before," Annette says, "it would be the same thing at any hotel in San Juan. They're all staffed by Teamsters. What good would it do to move to another one?"

"No good," Mike agrees. "That's why I want to put you in a safer place."

"What did you have in mind?" asks Jim.

"There's a house I know of, for rent. I pass it every day. It's on my block. And believe me, I live in a safe neighborhood. Private security patrol, gated community. Half the people who live there are either police officials, politicians, or corporate execs. It's got to be the safest neighborhood in San Juan."

Jim lets that settle. He looks at Annette, and the thought of her safety starts to tip him.

"I don't know. Maybe. What's it like?"

"Very nice. Midcentury modern, very stylish. Fully furnished. Comes with a housekeeper, and I've heard she's a great cook as well."

"Well…" Jim is hoping to find some flaw to turn it down. "How far is it from the office?"

"Ten-minute drive. And I should know. Like I said, I live on the same block, so I know exactly how easy it is to get to your office. Plus, I'm nearby, just in case…" He looks over at Annette who is smiling about this last part.

"Well, I don't know… Is it air-conditioned?" Jim asks, his resistance failing.

"Of course, it is," Mike says. Then he throws in his hole card. "Oh, and did I mention it has a really nice swimming pool? In case that interests you."

Jim hears that, and he caves, "I guess it's worth taking a look…"

Finally, the waitress returns.

Annette looks at hers, not quite as dark as usual, tastes it. "Kinda light on the double rum. Tell Tony I'm disappointed."

"Oh, Tony's not working today," the waitress tells her.

"Really? Where is he?"

"He's off."

High-Rise Office Building
Up on the Roof

Call-Me-Tony isn't quite off yet, but he's getting closer to the edge every second. He fights back, or tries, but Kiko doesn't even need the two other thugs with him. He can handle Tony all by himself. Tony struggles, he shouts, he begs and pleads. He drags his feet, leaving trails in the gravel on the flat roof. He even tries to bite Kiko, which earns him a vicious fist to the side of his head and knocks him cold.

This pisses Kiko off. He's looking forward to the expression of terror on Tony's face when he dangles him over the edge, staring at a twenty-story fall. Now the rat won't even know he's being tossed off the roof.

Kiko reaches the edge and pauses, holding up the limp, unconscious body. His two minions exchange a look. Whatever is stopping Kiko, they know it isn't reluctance to throw a man to his death. Kiko gives Tony a couple of slaps.

"Hey! You! Wake up!"

Nothing. Tony remains as limp in his arms as a plastic trash bag filled with Jell-O. Kiko thinks about sending his men to fetch a cup of water to throw in Tony's face and wake him up…but…

"Ah, fuck it," Kiko mutters.

He drops Tony over and watches all the way down until the man's body splats onto the concrete sidewalk far below.

37

Rental Bungalow
San Juan

IT's A GATED community, all right, with a double set of iron gates, which can be used as a sally port. A guard in a booth controls the opening and closing of the gates. The thing that Jim finds a little discomforting, though, is the other two guards, who both carry automatic weapons. There is something a bit too authoritarian about the look of military-grade security, almost un-American. And although at times it can slip his mind, Puerto Rico is part of the United States, and its people are American citizens.

But once they are inside the compound, that oppressive martial tone at the entry gates gives way to an atmosphere that seems like a suburban stereotype, almost a *Father Knows Best / Brady Bunch* kind of vibe. The idea of the Green Zone in Baghdad is still decades in the future. But the feeling of this almost-twilight-zone sense of total separation from the rest of the city and its people is still a bit unsettling.

Even as they pull up to the bungalow, the tall iron bars of the driveway gates add to the intimidation factor. The entire yard is itself enclosed in a ten-foot-high stucco fence, with the additional discouragement of broken glass embedded in the top of the wall. It almost feels like moving into a fortress. Or a prison.

But then they see the house.

As an architectural work, the house is simply stunning: redwood siding and flagstone; a low, sloped roof with greatly oversized overhangs that shade the plentiful windows; bold angles; an atrium inviting you to the front door within; and with wings of the house wrapped around the manicured courtyard. Inside the modern open floor plan makes the modest house seem larger than it looks from outside. There are three bedrooms, one for Jim, one for Annette, and a third which can serve as a convenient in-home office. It has an additional small studio apartment that serves the live-in help.

But what draws Jim through the open living room to the patio doors and then outside is the sparkling swimming pool, which features an extension, an arm six feet across, adding an extra forty feet to make swimming laps a pleasure.

"Right," he says, "We'll take it."

Annette scowls at his back and mutters, "Thanks for asking." But she turns to Mike Peralta and the realtor and says, "I think we can make it work."

She throws a quick, unexpected hug around Mike then steps back and turns away, hoping they believe she is looking out at the pool while her reddened cheeks burn, but there is a smile on her face.

Next, the realtor introduces Lettie, the housekeeper/cook, who is a permanent live-in whether the house has tenants or not. She is a fireplug of a woman, short and wide, but not at all soft-looking. In fact, her arms and shoulders look so solid you can imagine her lifting the couch with one hand to vacuum underneath it. She could be forty, she could be sixty. Her iron gray hair is wrapped in a tight bun, the coppery complexion of her face shows few lines, and the only real sign of age is around her deep-brown eyes.

They check out of the Hilton by phone and have one of the office gofers pick up their already-packed luggage and bring it to the house. The rumors of Lettie's cooking prowess prove to be understated. They turn in early, stuffed.

38

Crystal Towers Office Plaza
Law Office

WHILE THE INTERVIEW room is being set up for today's witnesses, Jim ducks into his corner office and puts through a call to Julie.

"Hi, sweetheart."

The buoyancy of his wife's voice immediately lifts him as her warm pleasure at the call magically travels through the wires all the way from Wisconsin, "Oh, Jim. I'm glad you called. Just in time, I'm meeting Betty for tennis at that new indoor club up in River Hills."

"That sounds great. I can't wait to see the place."

"Are you coming home soon?"

"Well… It doesn't look like this will wrap up any time soon, no."

"Oh… I guess I jumped to conclusions."

"What do you mean?"

"Well, I called the Hilton earlier, and they said you had checked out."

"Just did, yes. Moved."

"Moved to where?"

"Remember that FBI station chief I told you about?"

"Mike something, right?"

"Peralta. Great guy. He told us about a house for rent on his block. Very reasonable, although I could care less how much it costs Ron Cunningham."

"What made you decide that?"

"Oh, and it has a terrific pool. Did I tell you that? And a live-in housekeeper and chef who makes Julia Child look like a chuck-wagon cook."

"Then you better keep busy in that pool. I told you not to bother coming home fat."

"Don't worry. The pool is great. I've already used it twice. Last night and again early this morning."

"You're ducking my question."

"I'm... What..."

"Why did the FBI man find you a safehouse?"

"Jewel. It's not a 'safehouse.'"

"You live down the block from the FBI, and you're saying the house isn't safe? I'm not sure I buy that."

"No, of course it's safe. All I mean is, it's a very comfortable switch. Peace and quiet. Plenty of privacy."

"Jim, I just have one thing to ask you. Please."

"Sure, sure. What?"

"This time, listen to them."

"Who?"

"The FBI! Do what they tell you. Not like in Las Vegas, please. I can't stand to—"

"Jewel. It's okay. I promise, really. I am listening. Mike said he didn't like us living in a hotel, where all the staff are Teamsters. So we moved. An abundance of caution. You should see this new place. Gates. Armed guards. It would take a platoon of Marines to get through."

Julie doesn't answer right away. "I'm glad you have a safer place to stay. I'm not so thrilled that the FBI thinks you need one."

"They also have people on us. Just to be extra safe. Nothing can happen. Really."

Quiet. Then in a cooler voice she says, "I really do need to get going. You know Betty. She'll go nuts if we waste one minute of the hour of court time we paid for."

"Let me give you the new house phone. Thank God there was already service. It can take months to get them to turn on a phone here. Got a pencil?"

As he hangs up, Annette sticks her head in. "Got a sec?"

"Sure. What's up?"

"There's a rumor going around over in geek alley…" She nods out into the office, meaning to indicate the area where the technical team is located. "Are we setting up some kind of experiment?"

"Oh, damn. I am so sorry. Yes, and I want you to watch over the whole process. I messed up. With the guy in the dumpster and moving, it slipped my mind."

"What kind of experiment?"

"More of a scientific demonstration, really. I mean, it's not like we don't know what will happen. We just want to film it in a lab so there won't be any doubt in a jury's mind what kind of poison comes out of that urethane."

"So this is something we'll set up in a lab?"

"Exactly. I've done it before. Very powerful evidence."

"What exactly is it we're going do?"

"Well, the design is really up to the team. And you, of course. But the idea is pretty straightforward. We make a contained burn area."

"Contained how?"

"Usually, they set up some kind of maze thing. Wood walls. A clear top, like Lucite, so we can see inside. We can watch the rats. They're are free to move around, explore the maze. Then we introduce the smoke from burning urethane and just film what happens to them."

"Well, that's obvious," Annette says. "They die."

"Exactly. That's the point."

"Wait. You're doing this just to film the rats dying?"

"Have you ever watched what happens to a jury when two scientific experts start to debate each other over their facts and theories?"

"No. I suppose they go to sleep."

"They do indeed. Some of them believe us when we say this stuff will kill you. And some listen to the other side's expert. But they don't really understand a thing either one is saying."

"So you don't tell them, you show them."

"It demonstrates in real time just how fast and deadly that smoke is."

"No, I get it. You put the rats in the showers and then turn on the Zyklon B. I'm sure it makes very compelling cinema."

"It proves what we need to prove. Leaves no doubt. The jury doesn't forget that."

"About that? I'm sure you're right."

Two days later, the lab space is rented, the maze is completed, and the video cameras are all in position. Among other improvements, Annette has added a clock, like a stopwatch, in the upper-left corner of the maze so that as the process is filmed, the viewer sees the seconds tick by. Jim is very involved with his technical team, going over calculation models, showing how fast the toxic fumes will build up and then how long the effects will take to kill the rats.

Annette watches the six white lab rats in their cage, running on the wheel, drinking from the water bottle, gnawing on pellets.

One of the techs comes over and talks to the rats, "Okay, fellas. Time for all the players to strut their stuff on stage." He nods to Annette.

She picks up the cage and brings it over near the maze and says to Jim, "The cast is here. They're ready for their close-up, Mr. DeMille."

Jim turns to one of the techies and tells him, "Go ahead and load them in. I think three will be fine."

"Saving the other three in case we need to 'take two'?"

Jim nods and turns to the camera operator and says, "Let's get about five minutes of footage with them just moving around before we introduce the smoke."

Annette checks her watch and tells him, "I'll be back in two. Gotta make a phone call first."

"Don't be long," Jim says.

"I won't," she says.

She steps into the lab office and closes the door for privacy. She picks up the phone and dials.

39

Rental Bungalow
San Juan

WHEN THEY GET back to their house, Annette seems surprised how drained Jim appears. She recalls, back at the lab, how flawlessly the first demonstration they record goes. They watch the video playback. It's really graphic, the way the rats are fit and active until the smoke enters the maze. Within ten seconds, they are down. A few spasms, and it's over. They are stiff and dead in less than half a minute.

"Wow," Annette says. "What a horrible…"

"Thank God we got it in one take," Jim says, and she can hear in his voice how relieved he is.

That he is actually moved, disturbed even, at taking a life, even if they are only lab rats, she realizes how hard it was for him and respects him for the strength it took for him to go through with this because it's best for their case. But that's who he is, a man who will always go the extra mile.

But now, as they walk into their house, the toll on him is showing.

"You look beat," she says.

"I almost dread swimming my laps."

"So skip it. I won't tell."

"No. It will help me relax after all that." And he goes into his room to change into his swim trunks.

"That's one way," she shrugs and heads for the wet bar at the far side of the living room.

Jim has only been swimming for five minutes when the phone rings. She hurries over to the extension and picks it up.

She expects a call and answers with an eager, "Hello?"

"Hello?" It's not what she expects. Instead, she hears a woman's voice, but not familiar to Annette. Then the woman continues, "I'm calling to speak with Jim Feller, please."

"He's occupied right now."

"Not still working, I hope."

"No, actually. He's swimming."

"Don't bother him then. Just tell him Julie called. I'll talk to him tomorrow."

"Julie..." Then the penny drops. "Oh, Julie. Of course. This is Annette. I'm sorry, I didn't know your voice. Nice to meet you. Electronically."

"Same here. A pleasure. Jim must be working you to death, I imagine."

"No, not really. I'm something of a workaholic myself. Worse than he is, actually."

"No wonder he thinks you're so marvelous. You're as crazy as he is."

"I can give just about anybody a run for their money on that score."

"He really does think the world of you, though."

"That's very..." Annette stops, surprised how touched she is. "Thank you."

"Not at all," says Julie. "You deserve to hear it. And I know he'd never say anything."

"Well...I feel very lucky to work with him. He's quite amazing."

"Are you sure I can't go get him? I'd hate for him to miss your call."

"You'd hate it more if he misses his swim. Believe me."

"Well, I'll take your word for it. And again, nice to hear your voice. I hope we'll actually meet face-to-face soon."

"So do I… I told Jim I could come down in a few weeks when we go on spring break. I teach school, you know."

"I'll look forward to that."

"So, tell me," Julie says. "How bad is it?"

"It's a lot of work, but—"

"No, dear. I'm talking about the Teamsters. He won't tell me, but I'm sure that's the reason you two are practically in witness protection. Is he being…is he careful?"

"I can't… Look, I know they're a rough bunch and all, but…"

"They're murdering thugs, my dear. Don't ever forget it. And make sure Jim doesn't either. Don't let him take any chances."

"I will. I mean, I won't. Promise. And we're very safe, now that we've moved out of the hotel. This place is like a fortress."

"Yes. That's what worries me…"

Annette is about to tell her not to worry, but she knows that won't do any good. She also knows there's reason enough to worry.

"I'm going to keep him out of trouble. I'll keep him on a short leash."

"Good luck with that, dear. Good night."

About ten seconds after she hangs up, the phone rings again. She picks it up on the first ring.

"Hello."

"I tried calling before. Your line was busy."

"I'm very popular. Are you coming over?"

"See you soon." The phone goes dead.

When Jim comes inside, Annette wonders if she should ask him if he wants to join them for a drink.

But before she can speak, he says, "That's it. I am totally beat. I'm going to bed before I crash and burn." So she just says good night and doesn't mention anything else.

Jim wades through eight inches of black water, which laps against the sides of the foundation. He picks his way carefully to avoid stepping on any invisible hazard hidden in the filthy, soot-laden water, stepping between the charred studs where a wall used to be. The firemen were just hosing out the last embers when he arrived. They didn't want to let him into the structure, but he pulled on waders and did it anyway. His flashlight beam plays over the burnt wreckage of the basement den. He knows he's being stupid, coming in here. This isn't even a case. Although maybe it will be. But that's not why he insisted on going in as soon as possible. This is Fred McMichael's house. It's only three houses down the street from his own. As he watched it burn, he finally got an answer to the question he kept asking, "Did Fred make it out?"

He didn't.

Jim's flashlight beam finds the charred frame of a couch, the one Fred liked to lie on, reading mysteries and smoking. Jim expects there won't be any big mystery about the origin of this fire. He sweeps the light around.

There's Fred. He floats face down in the black water, but Jim knows it wasn't drowning that killed him. He stops, standing there. Up on ground level, the fire crew is making all kinds of noise. One of them is shouting at him to get up out of there or he's going to be arrested.

But Jim isn't listening. All he hears is the lap of the water against the foundation as he stares at the floating body.

Jim isn't sure what wakes him. But something. A sound? A voice? Still as stone, he listens, trying to pick up any sound that might tell him what's wrong. Is there someone else in the house? He tries to brush the thought away, but now that it's in his head, that's impossible. He rises silently from his bed, gliding to the door to open it a crack and listen, but he hears only one thing at the edge of the silence. The gentle lap of water. At first, he thinks it's a lingering illusion from his nightmare, but then it hits him. It must be the pool. Is someone in the pool? It's hard to tell.

Quietly as he can, he creeps from his room, moving through the darkened house to the living room. As he stands there, stock still, that lapping water out at the pool is the only sound. He blocks out the image that leaps into his mind. Annette, dead, floating facedown. He wants to charge out to the pool, wants to call out Annette's name, but caution tells him not to reveal himself. If someone else is in the house, he wants to know that before he moves. He strains to hear anything else.

Slowly, cautiously, as he slinks through shadows, as he gets closer to the patio doors, he can see more of the actual surface of the pool. Annette is in there, all right.

He turns just in time to see the form of a large man step out of the hall.

As Jim jumps, a shout escapes him, "Woah!"

The big shadowy man jumps at the same time, screaming, "Jesus!"

"Mike? Is that you?"

"Christ, Jim. You scared the hell out of me."

"Me? You almost gave me a heart attack."

Then a light flips on. "What the hell are you two yelling about?" Dripping pool water on the floor, Annette is shaking her head.

"Oh, crap," Jim mumbles. "Mike, I'm sorry. I thought you were…" He trails off, not sure what to say. "What are you doing here?"

"Annette invited me over for a swim. Anything wrong with that?"

"No," Jim manages. "Not a thing." He gives Annette a weak smile.

"We're consenting swimmers, Dad. If you don't mind."

Jim scrambles to his feet, his face reddened as he scrambles for the door to his bedroom. "Sorry, sorry. You two go right ahead…"

"Thanks for your blessing." She takes Mike by the arm and whispers a question to him that Jim can't hear.

He's up early, but the smell of frying bacon is already calling to him from the kitchen. Their housekeeper is at the stove, working magic. Out on the patio, Annette and Mike sit in a pair of wicker lounge chairs, pulled close together. He smiles. Clearly they managed to overcome the trauma of their interruption last night.

"Morning," he calls. "If you lovebirds can't tear yourselves apart and come inside, I'm going to eat all the bacon."

40

Interview Room
Crystal Towers Office Plaza

As soon as Jim and Annette reach the office, one of the researchers, Martin Flores, tells them a witness he's been hunting down has come in voluntarily this morning, a walk-in. His name is Luis Ortiz.

He begins with an apology for ducking them, "I was afraid. But when I heard about what happened to Tony Nogueras?" He shakes his head. "We used to work together at the Sheraton. They knocked it down years ago, put up the new one. Anyway, Tony... I mean, that was a guy who tried to keep clear of any union stuff. Never stuck his nose into nobody else's business. If those bastards would go after him? I figure nobody is safe anyway. I might as well come in and tell what I saw."

He starts by explaining, or more accurately, confessing the affair he was having with Sofia, ashamed to admit that this was another reason he wanted to keep out of the investigation. He didn't want to open that up.

"What good would it do?" he says as he starts to break down. "She's gone. They killed her, sure as if they shot her. Or threw her off a roof."

"She was one of the fire victims then?" Annette asks gently. "I'm very sorry for your loss."

Luis wipes his eyes on his sleeve, composes himself. "Effie. My wife? She's a good woman, a good mother. I don't want her to learn of this...thing with Sofia. It would kill her."

Jim looks Luis in the eye. "Señor Ortiz, what you tell us is confidential, but only to a point. I have to be honest with you about that. If this matter ends up in court, you might be called as a witness."

"No, I understand that. But I have made up my mind. I have to tell what I saw. I can't live with this thing weighing on my heart." And Luis picks up his story. "Sofia and me, we went into the pantry together. It's a big space."

"Yes, we've seen the entire hotel. We know the room."

"We were in the back when I hear this squeaking. And I know this sound. It's one of the rolling carts. That damn wheel, it always... Anyway. When this guy rolls the cart into the pantry—"

"Did you know who it was?" Annette cuts in, excited.

Jim holds up a hand, admonishing her. "I'm sorry about the interruption. But as long as we've stopped you... could you identify the man?"

"Hell, yes. I know him for years. It's Efrain Rosa. He works in the kitchen. Butcher. Thinks he's a big shot with the union too."

Jim and Annette exchange a knowing look. "Okay, Rosa comes into the pantry with the cart. What did you see next?"

"He started pulling stuff off the shelves. We could only hear it at first, couldn't see what it was. Little cans, it sounded like. But we stayed hidden until he was gone. Then we went over to the shelf where he took stuff. I wanted to know what the bastard was stealing."

"And could you tell what was missing?"

"Yeah. About twenty cans of Sterno."

When the interview ends, Jim cautions Luis to keep his eyes open, just in case. Ortiz says he is going away with his wife, who is from out in the country. He has given up on working in hotels. Maybe he'll open a little restaurant. On the way out, he leaves contact information so they can find him again.

They call Mike. He tells Jim that the San Juan Police have located Rosa. Mike now has Rosa under surveillance. He doesn't want to arrest him yet—that would tip off the other conspirators—but they are closing in on this case.

41

Day Drinker's Cantina
San Juan

THE BAR HAS a name, but nobody uses it. Everybody just calls it Day Drinker's. It's dark, it's cheap, and the hardcore patrons know enough to leave you the hell alone here. That's fine with Kiko.

Yesterday he put the pressure on Cora again, "People tell me they seen you drinking with our friend."

"Who?"

"Freddy. You remember your friend, Freddy Vázquez. You were going to let me know if he turned up."

"I would have. I just ran into him. But I don't know where he's staying or nothing. So there was nothing to tel—"

Again, that thumb-digging, blinding him with pain.

"Have you ever done a jigsaw puzzle, Jorge?"

"What? No. Well, with my kids, maybe."

"It's all a big mess before you start. Can't tell a thing about it."

"Okay, but—"

"But once you put all the pieces together, it all comes clear. Understand?

"Sure, I…guess."

"When I tell you to let me know if you see Freddy, I am gathering my puzzle pieces. I didn't ask you to solve the fucking puzzle. Did I?"

"No…"

"All I ask is that you help me gather the pieces. Every little thing people tell me? I'm the one who puts them together. So you don't decide if I need to know something or not. You never know what piece I'm looking for."

"Okay, I'm sorr—" Cora buckles to his knees as the thumb sends his nerve into total shock.

"Where?"

"I said, I don't know where he is."

"I'm asking where he was. I can take it from there."

The trail wasn't very long. Freddy practically lives at the Day Drinker's. It's much easier to find him here than to run into him at home. Kiko only has to wait for an hour and a half. And here's Freddy.

The guy looks bad enough that he could be stumbling out of the bar instead of just arriving. Kiko can smell him halfway across the room. When Freddy finally lays his yellowing, bloodshot eyes on Kiko, there is a short circuit that lasts a second before he registers who it is.

Then his expression changes, but the look on his face is not that stab of fear Kiko expects. Instead of terror, he sees Freddy relax in a posture that can only be relief. He's ready for it to be over.

Yesterday, after Kiko comes to see him, Jorge Cora decides to take some time off work. In fact, he decides he might just look for a new occupation, someplace where he won't have to be a member in good standing of the International Brotherhood of Teamsters, Local 901. And when he thinks about that, he realizes there is only one way this is going to happen. First, he must figure out a way he can manage to stay alive long enough.

When Martin Flores tells Jim there's a witness on the phone who insists he needs to talk right now, he says okay, put him through.

"Who is it?" he asks Flores.

"His name is Cora. We've already seen him, but—"

Jim and Annette exchange a smile. He picks up the line and puts it on speaker phone.

42

Rental Bungalow
San Juan

THINGS MOVE QUICKLY once they talk to Cora. He refuses to come to their office. When he tells them why—the camera trained on their elevator—they are in shock. But quickly Mike Peralta coordinates with local police to pay a call on the Teamsters auxiliary office, the one across Calle Mille Flores, with the video camera. But that horse has left the barn, and they realize a lot of damage has been done.

Cora still refuses to come in to the office though. He knows they moved out of the Hilton. He insists on meeting them at the rental house. If it's safe enough for them…

Mike Peralta sends a car with two agents to pick Cora up. When they arrive with him at the house, everyone sits down around the dining-room table. Mike tells his two agents, Forshay and Littleton, to stick around. He wants them watching the house. Just in case.

On his way over, in the car with the agents, Cora hears a radio call coming in. San Juan PD confirms identity of the body discovered in an alley an hour ago. The deceased is Freddy Vázquez. Apparent cause of death is multiple knife wounds. Cora takes the news in stride. He knows Kiko has taken care of a loose end. He's terrified, but it's almost satisfying, as this helps him justify his decision to turn rat. He is proud of himself. He knew Kiko would go after Freddy. But Cora didn't wait around. He's making his move already before he even knows Freddy is dead. This puts him a step ahead. He knows he's a loose end too, and he's not waiting around.

The Jorge Cora who sits down doesn't seem to be even a distant relative of the cocky, confident, young man they interviewed before. If she didn't know better, Annette thinks, she wouldn't know it was the same punk. The dark circles under his eyes, the booze on his breath, the fingernails bitten to the quick speak for themselves. But it is the fear inside that strains to show out. His eyes dart around like a frightened bird. His leg jiggles, his hands shake, he can't seem to overcome the dryness in his throat, even after his third glass of water.

Mike Peralta does the questioning this time. He cautions Cora, tells him his rights. Mike has authority from the US attorney to hear Cora's proffer. In exchange for Cora's complete cooperation, he will consider providing protection and immunity. He offers to furnish Cora with a lawyer.

"Nah. Just don't throw me to the wolves, that's all."

"So you understand," Mike says. "This is an official FBI interview as part of an investigation of murder, racketeering, arson, and conspiracy. You are cautioned that lying to the FBI is a felony. You understand that?"

Cora's leg is jiggling up and down so violently it shakes the table. "Yeah, yeah. Fine. How do we do this? You ask questions, or what?"

"We'll start with a few questions. You told us before that you attended the union meeting on the day of the fire. At that time, were you aware of any plans to disrupt the meeting?"

"Yes. Oh, yeah, that was us…" And he goes on to describe the way they staged the fight and got the riot going, with the intent to distract the guards.

"Who planned this disruption?"

"All of them. Us, I mean. Together."

"Can you tell us where this planning took place?"

"We had a meeting. At the Hilton, in the lounge."

Jim and Annette exchange a short whisper. Jim speaks quietly into Mike's ear.

Mike nods and picks up the questioning, "Can you give us the names of the people attending this meeting?"

"You people, you have to swear you're going to protect me, yeah? Because if I tell you this, I am a dead man."

"We're aware you're taking a grave risk, and we are prepared to provide you protection accordingly. But this depends on your level of cooperation. If we find out you are lying or holding out, then the deal is off, and you're on your own."

"Fine, I ain't gonna hold nothing back. Okay. So we meet up at the Hilton. To talk about how to put some pressure on the hotel people."

"Again, can you identify for us the individuals present?"

"You mean, who's at this meeting? Me. Freddy Vázquez, who they killed already. Him and me, we started that fight. Then there was Efrain Rosa and Wilfredo Torres. They're the ones who started the fire. And Kiko Cabrera, he helped start the riot. He's the main muscle for Beltran."

"Roberto Beltran, the president of Local 901?"

"Right. Him."

"And you're saying Beltran was at this meeting at the Hilton?"

"Of course, he was there. He's the one gave us the green light to go ahead with the plan to start a fire."

Cora gives them everything, even admits Kiko paid him to start that little fire by the pool at the Hilton to put a scare into Jim. He confirms it was Rosa who tried to start a fire in the linen closet before Christmas, but he screwed it up. That's when Beltran decided the need to kick it up a notch.

"But not to kill all those people," he insists. "Nobody wanted that."

"Arson that results in manslaughter is considered homicide," Mike says flatly. "You can't put a loaded gun to someone's head and pull the trigger then say you just wanted to get his attention."

"Yeah, sure. I just… We didn't know. That's all I want to say."

When they finish, they leave Cora inside with the two FBI agents guarding him and adjourn to the patio to confer by the pool.

"He's terrified, that's obvious. I believe him," Annette says, then asks, "What do you think, Mike?"

"He's too scared to lie. And everything lines up with what you got from that guy in the kitchen. Ortiz, was it?"

"Yes," Jim says. "We were pretty sure about Rosa already. He got the Sterno. And Torres, the guy with the keys? It all fits."

"And Call-Me-Tony'," Annette says. "They knew about him from their damn camera. I can't believe we... They knew about everyone. I got Tony to cooperate, and then they killed him. His death is on me." Mike steps forward to put his arm around her. But she steps back, shaking her head. "No, don't. I screwed up."

Jim, too, wants to comfort her, "With all my experience, that's a new one on me. I never figured the glass elevator. I should have figured that out. The blame falls on my shoulders not yours."

He looks at Mike. "You have enough to act on?"

Mike nods. "It's time to round these people up before they go after anyone else."

Mike already has a coordinated arrest plan worked out. Rosa is under surveillance already, and the San Juan PD has located Torres. Beltran is at union headquarters, and Kiko is there with him.

"It's time to drop the hammer," Mike says.

"I assume you're going after Beltran yourself," Jim says.

"Wouldn't miss that one for the world."

"Neither would I. You know that, right?"

"Would it do any good to say no to you?"

"You could say no. But you'd have to arrest me too."

"Then I guess I won't say no."

Annette clears her throat, feeling like she may choke on all the testosterone fumes, then says, "You know I'm going with you, right?"

Mike turns to her. "I can't let you do that."

"Oh, bullshit, Mike. Don't pull your Latin macho crap on me."

"He doesn't have to," Jim says. "I'm exercising my rights as a crusty, old, Midwestern, chauvinist pig."

"You think you can stop me?"

"I think I can fire you. And I'd hate to do that."

"Really? You'd pull that kind of stuff?"

"It's pulled. Besides, I need you to keep working on Cora."

Mike jumps in, saying, "I'm leaving Forshay and Littleton with you. They can do the interviewing, but you direct them on what to ask. Keep him busy, make sure he doesn't take off into the wind."

"He's not going anywhere. The guy's falling apart."

"Perfect," Jim says. "You can keep him talking and pick his bones clean. I know you can do it. I'm counting on it."

Annette thinks that's just a bullshit excuse to leave her behind. But she knows Jim well enough by now to take him seriously about firing her. She doesn't like it, but she accepts it anyway.

"Fine. You big boys just ride off with the posse and leave the little gal safe back here on the ranch. Maybe I'll bake you a pie or something."

"You can ask Lettie to do that," Jim teases. "How often do you have your own personal chef?"

Annette smiles at that. "Fine. Get out of here, both of you."

43

Teamster Headquarters
San Juan

MIKE SETS HIS tactical units in place, one to cover the rear of the building, one to go in the front door with him. Jim feels the sweat on his chest and back. The damn Kevlar vest is heavy and hot in the late San Juan afternoon. The half-dozen agents ready to lead the way into the Teamster building look like they are launching a military assault.

"Ready?" Mike asks him.

"Yup." He nods at the heavily armed squad. "You don't think this whole SWAT thing is a little bit of overkill?"

"I certainly hope so."

"I mean, do you really expect a fight here?"

"Hell, no. That's why we put on the show." Mike grins. "Besides, I need overwhelming force to make up for my greatest weakness here. You."

"Aw. I'm touched, Mike."

"Don't be. I'm only doing it for Annette. She'd kill me if you get hurt."

On Mike's command, the force moves with the smooth precision of the New England Patriots on a third and three. They are through the door and across the office faster than you could say it. One SWAT officer stays back, holding his weapon loosely over the terrified office workers, who all hit the deck at his demand, lying on bellies, hands behind their heads.

Mike leads the rest through the utility room, rolling up on the office in the back, where Roberto Beltran stands stock still, hands raised high in unmistakable surrender.

As he is being cuffed, Beltran looks at Jim, smiling as he asks Mike, "Where are you taking me? Federal building? I want to know where my lawyer should go."

Mike ignores him, turning to his squad leader. "Did you find Cabrera?"

"No, sir. Not yet."

"Kiko isn't here," Beltran says. "And before you ask, I have no idea where he is."

44

Rental Bungalow
San Juan

AGENT FLOYD LITTLETON has his service weapon handy as he makes another sweep of the yard's perimeter. Probably overkill, he thinks, but it's the kind of proactive approach to protective duty. But between the armed guards at the neighborhood's only entry point and the ten-foot fence surrounding the rental house property, Littleton doesn't expect to find anyone lurking.

And he is right about that. Kinda.

As he opens the front door, Littleton can smell a pie in the oven. He thought Jim was kidding about having a live-in cook, but it's true, and that pie smells really good.

"All clear out there," he calls out to Forshay, who's sitting on the couch with his back to Littleton. "When's the pie gonna be ready?" he asks.

But Agent Forshay remains silent, and just as the thought that his partner is sitting as still as death hits him, Kiko has the piano-wire garrote around Littleton's neck. As his vision begins to go black, Littleton glances toward the kitchen. This time, instead of noticing the smell of pie, he sees the cook. She's on the floor in a pool of blood. Then Littleton's world goes black.

A minute earlier, while Littleton is outside on his patrol, Kiko enters through a bedroom window. This whole plan is fucked up already. He intended to plant a bomb in the lawyer's car and be long gone when he started it up and blew himself to kingdom come. But when he reaches the bungalow, he can see through the high iron driveway gate that the car is gone.

So he comes in through the window and creeps into the hall. He listens, trying to place the people inside the house. He hears someone rattling in the kitchen. The cook. The pie smells good.

Voices in the living room…or is it the dining room? Silently he ghosts down the hall. The garrote is set just so in his pocket so he can snatch it out in an instant. In his hand now is the seven-inch hunting knife he carries in the hand-tooled leather sheath on his belt. He moves to the end of the hall and peers into the living room. Nobody. But in the dining room beyond, there's Cora, sitting at a table with that lawyer lady, spilling his guts, the *maricon*. But where's the other FBI agent? The sound of the toilet flushing in the bathroom just behind him tips him off, and he is ready when the bathroom door opens.

Agent Forshay is faster than Kiko expects. His gun has already cleared his holster as Kiko's blade rams into his heart. The gun hits the floor with a clatter. Loud. Did the others hear that? The FBI agent has his mouth open, but he can't quite get the breath to cry out. And then the urge to warn them is itself gone as the blood which should be pumping to his brain stops along with his heart. Kiko is holding him as the light goes out from his eyes. Silently he lowers the agent's body to the floor.

Now Kiko listens again. He feels lucky when he hears the lawyer lady still talking with the rat. He will shut them both up.

They don't hear him as he steps out of the hall. His movement is as silent as Death itself. He decides to take out Cora first. Kill the man. Then if the woman puts up resistance, she will be easier to finish than a man would be. He moves past the entry to the kitchen, his eyes on Cora.

When he feels the blade jam into his lower back, he bellows in pain. He feels the blade pull out, and before he can be stabbed again, instinct guides his reaction. He whirls to see a sixty-year-old woman holding a paring knife. It's short, maybe two and a half, three inches. But that is his blood on the first inch of the blade.

As he slashes out with his own knife, the old cook steps back, and he barely nicks her belly. But instead of screaming or trying to run, she strikes again with her little knife, and he feels a hot tear open up in his forearm.

But now he sees that his cry of pain from the first wound brings Cora and the woman to their feet. They start to run for the hall, probably to get into a bedroom where they can try to hold him off. Maybe there's a weapon back there.

But before he can do anything about going after them, Kiko needs to finish this old bat with the knife. He lunges, she dodges, she slashes, he counters to avoid the blade. Then he uses the advantage of longer arms to stab, and his blade plunges deep. He twists the knife as he pulls it out and draws it back to stab again. He doesn't expect it when the old woman steps forward and jams that little knife into his side. But her grip falters, and she loses hold of her little paring knife, leaving it sticking out of Kiko's side. He rams his knife deep into her chest again and shoves her as he pulls it out. She staggers, slips on blood, and crashes to the floor. He pulls the little knife out of his side, wincing at the annoying pain. He doesn't take time to watch her die.

Turning toward the hall, he hears a bedroom door slam shut. He can even hear the click of the lock. Fine. They have nowhere to go. Ignoring the pain of his bleeding wounds, Kiko stalks after them, into the hall. He is just about to step over the dead FBI man and knock the door down when his feral instincts alert him that something is wrong. He knows immediately what it is. The gun. The FBI man's gun was lying right out on the floor. Now it's gone.

His hesitation gives him a moment to consider. The pair in the bedroom will have it pointed at the door, ready to blast the first thing that comes through. He can probably take them anyway, gun or not. But that will have to wait. Right now his biggest worry is that second FBI. He will come back inside any moment.

Kiko will need a distraction, something to draw the agent's attention when he first comes in the door so Kiko can get behind him.

He drags Forshay, the dead FBI agent, from the hall into the living room. The man is a big fucker, he thinks. It costs Kiko in blood and pain to move the dead weight. But he grits through and stages the body on the couch. Propped, sitting up, the back of his head will be the first thing his partner sees when he opens the door. It only needs to work for a second, just enough to get behind him.

Kiko sheaths his knife and draws the garrote from his pocket, two feet of piano wire, with wood handles on either end.

Jim finds it odd that there are no armed guards at the compound gate. There isn't even a man in the booth to work the gate. He calls out. No answer. He doesn't like it. They may be back in thirty seconds for all he knows. But something tells him not to wait. He gets out of the car and goes to the booth to open the gate himself. When he hits the control button, he sees a smear of blood on the guard's stool. He flies back into the car and guns it through the opening gate.

As Jim dashes headlong into the bungalow, he hears a loud crack from down the hall. It sounds like a closed door being crashed off the hinges. As he runs into the hall, he hears a gunshot.

Annette feels the weight of the FBI agent's gun heavy in her hand. It's starting to be a strain, holding it up, trained on the door.

"Here. Give me the gun," Cora says, trying to reach for it.

"Hands off!" she barks as him, and he stops himself.

Her arms are starting to tremble from the effort of holding the gun out and from the fear she is trying to ignore.

She is ready when the door explodes off the hinges. As Kiko barrels into the room, she squeezes off a shot. It tears a slab of meat off the big man's shoulder, and between his momentum into the door and the impact of being shot, Kiko crashes to the floor. But he isn't going to stay down. He is stunned, groggy, but is struggling to get back on his feet.

"Shoot him again!" Cora shouts.

But before she can decide to kill a man at close range, Cora grabs her and wrestles the gun away. By the time Cora gets a grip on the handle and fits his finger inside the trigger guard, Kiko hits him like a battering ram, and the gun goes flying.

Kiko squeezes his meat-hook hands around Cora's throat. He pins him against the wall, leaning into the choke hold. Then he removes the hand of his wounded arm but keeps choking Cora with the good hand.

Annette sees Cora's eyes bugging out. She scuttles across the floor and picks up the gun again. She levels it at Kiko, but she hesitates, afraid if she shoots, she will hit Cora.

"Let go!" she yells as she fires into the air, hoping to force Kiko to release his choke hold. He does.

Kiko turns on Annette instead, pulling his knife from the sheath with his good arm.

Jim jumps over the dead FBI man and dashes into the bedroom through the busted doorway. He is too late to stop Kiko, who is already charging at Annette with his great, bloody blade.

She stops him herself, squeezing off another round, this one aimed right at the charging thug's forehead. The explosion of bone, blood, and cerebral matter splatters the walls, the floor, and the trembling woman with the smoking gun in her hand.

Jim stares at the tableau before him: Cora, gasping on the floor, curled into the corner; Kiko on the floor, minus a couple quarts of blood and now about half his skull as well; and Annette, who is hyperventilating. She turns to look at Jim.

"Am I…" She swallows, trying to slow her heart. "Am I going to need a good lawyer?"

"I don't know. It's doesn't look like you need any help to me." Jim's nose wrinkles. If there's one smell Jim knows, it's smoke. "You smell something?"

Cora is on his feet now. "Oh, shit. The pie!"

PART FOUR

AFTERMATH

THE WEDDING TAKES place at Sailfish Point Resort, an hour up the coast from San Juan. The bride wears a gown handed down from her mother. Since Annette's father is deceased, James Feller, Esq. gives away the bride.

Mike Peralta, it turns out, has quite the extended family. Two uncles are federal judges, one in New Jersey, the other in Florida. His grandfather has a half-brother, twenty years his junior, who sits on the State Supreme Court in Connecticut. As for Mike's seven brothers, three are military officers, two are businessmen, one is a surgeon, and the last is a dentist. Mike's three sisters are all married; one's a lawyer, one is a psychologist, and the youngest is on maternal leave from her job in the State Department. He has more nieces and nephews than even he can remember. Although he does keep track of his sister's kid, Adolfo, a pitcher who just signed with the Florida Marlins.

Many of the guests fly in from the mainland, and most of these stay at the Sailfish, a four-star resort. But when Julie flies down, Jim surprises her with the magnificent villa he has rented on a point of land that commands almost a 360-degree view of the ocean. They don't need all six bedrooms, of course. But they do manage to fill five of them as the date of the wedding comes after summer break starts for Julie and Jim's girls. Ellen brings her new fiancé, Andrew, a graduate student in architecture who is also a champion tennis player, which pleases Julie to no end. Sarah brings a sorority sister, Hilary, which fills a third and fourth bedroom. But since Jim and Julie plan to stay there for six weeks, various guests, friends, and relations will shuttle in an out.

The outcome of the case, like any case, has its plusses and minuses. Thanks in part to the graphic power of the rat-poisoning video, the company which made the urethane foam filling for the furniture cushions settles with an amount that turns out to be almost 15 percent of the eventual costs. They feel lucky to get off so easy. Three years earlier, Jim nailed them hard on a prior case. So they are thrilled to get off so lightly. What's more, the video Jim has made becomes a part of the evidence Jim presents to a congressional hearing considering regulations on urethane. Eventually, a watered-down version makes it through in spite of the money spigot opened up by industry lobbyists. Better than nothing.

The furniture makers are also named, but Jim ends up dropping the claim against them. They refuse to pay anything, claiming that the urethane makers' settlement absolves them of any responsibility. Jim doesn't agree, but it isn't worth a court fight. A jury could easily take their side.

The architectural firm, the one which designs the exit doors for the casino, turns out to have designed them to open outward, as they should have. It was the contractor's crew who fails to follow the plans and installs them backward. However, the contractor's company is effectively judgment proof as they had already been driven out of business. As to the question of how this defective construction passes inspection in the first place, that is cleared up when it turns out the Building Code inspector's on the take. In fact, that's the factor that triggers the investigation which ends up closing down the contractor.

Mike Peralta turns over his criminal investigation to an organized-crime task force putting together a huge racketeering case against the Teamsters. As for the murders, those are outside of federal statutes. They're addressed in the criminal courts of Puerto Rico.

The two arsonists, Rosa and Torres, go to trial charged with ninety-seven counts of murder in the second degree. They are convicted and receive multiple life sentences without hope of parole. The judge is particularly harsh in sentencing because the defendants steadfastly refuse to offer any testimony, or even admit to any connection, linking Roberto Beltran or the Teamsters to the fire.

Beltran stands trial anyway, charged on the basis of testimony provided by Jorge Cora. As is his right under Puerto Rico statute, Beltran turns down having a jury trial. He elects, instead, to be tried before a judge only. This decision puts the sole power to acquit or convict directly in the hands a trial judge—a risky proposition usually, especially when there is credible evidence. A jury might be swayed, or even confused, by a good defense. But having a judge hear the case, one who knows the law much better than any jury, seems to be an odd choice. When Beltran is found innocent of the charges, there's a great outcry, accusations of bribery, etc. Nothing comes of it. Beltran gets off.

As for the civil litigation against the Teamsters for starting the fire, they get nailed big time, paying 65 percent of the damages from the fire, nearly two hundred million dollars.

Jim's client, the hotel, is held responsible for the locked doors and the construction defects. They end up paying out just over 20 percent of the damages, almost all of it to the survivors of guests or employees. It's a huge financial hit, but a better outcome than Jim expects and, in Annette's private opinion, better than they deserve.

The consortium of owners takes almost four years to complete the reconstruction and remodeling needed to reopen the hotel. It remains open for five years until it's purchased by a private equity group in 1998 and demolished to make room for a new resort. It is rumored that the loans which pay for this new resort come from the retirement funds of the International Brotherhood of Teamsters.

After he's found not guilty by the judge, Ricardo Beltran does not return to his position as president of Local 901. He remains with the Teamsters, an executive position with a nominal job title and very little responsibility. That's fine with him. Part of the reason is his health. He developed a chronic cough, which he always blamed on that goddamn black smoke. He thought about suing somebody, but no decent attorney was willing to take his case. After a couple years, his cough developed into emphysema and then full-on COPD.

Beltran knows how sick he is, and he will complain to anybody who listens. He is resentful over being so sick. Why him? What did he ever do? He gave everything to the Teamsters, everything, even his health. He never caves when they charge him, never rats out when prosecutors offer him deals. He keeps his mouth shut. He stands trial, and he's ready to do his time. He never admits anything and swears in court the Teamsters didn't do it. And fuck anybody who thinks there's a payoff. Beltran stays strong, a standup guy.

And now, look at him, a dying man. Where's the justice?

It's been a few years, but Jim and Mike still keep in touch. He doesn't like how often Jim sends Annette out on the road for months at a time. Of course, she is the best in the business, except for Jim, that is.

"Now you know why Julie makes me stay home."

"Makes you? Ha. You stuck my wife with all the hard work so you could sit around and play golf."

"Tennis."

"Whatever. I can't keep up with all that country-club stuff anyway."

"Is that why you called? Tennis is the one where you have a little fence between you, and you hit a bal—"

"Cut it out," Mike rumbles, but fighting not to laugh. "No, I called you to clear up a little 'old business' you might like to know about."

"Is this about sticking you with the check last time?"

"Beltran."

Jim shuts up. All ears now.

"Tell me what you've got."

"This is not for public knowledge, now."

"I'm sealed like a tomb. Attorney-client privilege."

"You're not my attorney."

"I won't tell if you won't."

"So. Okay then. Remember how Beltran was telling everyone how he was all sick? From smoke, he claims?"

"Don't tell me he finally found a lawyer to take that bullshit case?"

"No, no. You know I told you about that task force?"

"The one that's been talking a big game about the Teamsters for years now? That one?"

"I'll ignore that. Anyway, they got a wire on some of the top guys. And guess what they're all upset over?"

"Not the FBI, I'll wager."

"Still with a hard-on for Teamsters. You want to hear this or just bitch about the wheels of justice?"

"Well…I do like to bitch. But go ahead."

"Word has gone up the line, all the way, about poor Roberto Beltran being so sick and all. It raises concerns. After all, the guy is practically a dying man. And they worry, who knows what happens when a man knows he's going to meet his maker. A guy like this is susceptible to an attack of conscience. Who knows what he'll tell people? Maybe a confession to clear his soul or atone for his sins."

"Are you telling me Beltran is going to rat?"

"Him. Never. In fact, nobody has seen the guy in a month."

"Interesting. So the big boys see Beltran as a loose end."

"And you know the Teamsters," Mike says. "They don't like leaving any loose ends."

"Right," Jim says, a smile coming on. "Just ask Jimmy Hoffa."

ABOUT THE AUTHOR

LEE DION IS a naturalist and educator. He holds master's degrees in natural science and chemistry. He is an accomplished pilot, skier, sailor, scuba diver, golfer, tennis player, and a lifetime master bridge player. He has written several natural science articles and a short story. This is his first novel. He lives with his wife, Micki, in East Hampton, New York, and Piper's Landing, Florida.

CPSIA information can be obtained
at www.ICGtesting.com
Printed in the USA
BVHW081352071221
623424BV00003B/182